A CINDERELLA TO
SECURE HIS HEIR

A CINDERELLA TO SECURE HIS HEIR

MICHELLE SMART

MILLS & BOON

First published in Great Britain 2019
by Mills & Boon, an imprint of HarperCollins*Publishers*
1 London Bridge Street, London, SE1 9GF

Large Print edition 2019

© 2019 Michelle Smart

ISBN: 978-0-263-08271-5

MIX
Paper from
responsible sources
FSC
www.fsc.org
FSC™ C007454

Printed and bound in Great Britain
by CPI Group (UK) Ltd, Croydon, CR0 4YY

This is for the most loyal, loving creature on this earth, without whom I would probably never leave my office. My dog, Stewie! Xxx

CHAPTER ONE

BETH HARDINGSTONE ENTERED the arrivals department of Vienna International Airport, pushing Dom's pram with one hand and dragging her suitcase full of baby paraphernalia with the other. She looked around for the driver she'd been promised would meet her and hoped it wouldn't be too long before she could throw a mug of super-strong coffee down her throat. She needed caffeine, badly.

Dom was suffering with teething pains and had kept her up all night with his crying. She'd finally fallen asleep at silly o'clock, less than an hour before she'd had to get up and get ready for their early-morning flight to Vienna. There had been no chance of sleep on the plane. Dom had not enjoyed his first flight and had made sure every passenger knew it.

He was fast asleep now, though, flat on his back in his pram, thumb in mouth, as cherubic as it was possible to be.

People always said how hard the first year of babyhood was but until you'd lived it for yourself there was no way to appreciate the sheer hard work and exhaustion that went with it. There was also no way to appreciate the unremitting joy that went with it either: the gummy smiles, the gurgling laughs, the explosions of love that came from picking up a screaming child and having him immediately quieten from being held in your arms.

A tall figure leant against a wall caught her eye.

He looked up from the phone in his hand. As his eyes met hers, her heart made a sudden leap.

Six weeks ago, Beth had been offered the event manager's job of a lifetime—organising a Viennese masquerade ball. The Greek billionaire who'd bought a palace in Vienna and spent millions renovating it into an exclusive hotel for the filthy rich had sent his representative to deal with Beth's company on his behalf. That representative had been this man, Valente Cortada.

In her six years working at White's Events, where models of both sexes were regularly used as hosts and hostesses, where clients were rich and powerful, where guests were the staple of gossip columns, Beth had never met anyone who'd made her suck in a breath with one look as Valente had.

His instructions had been to secure Beth's agreement to run the masquerade ball. That she'd been at the time nine months into a year's unpaid leave and had no childcare arrangements in place had been overcome by Valente and her boss Lucinda setting her up with all the technology needed to organise things remotely from the comfort of Beth's flat, and providing her with all the staff needed to assist her. As the sleeping baby was the reason for her year's leave, and as she refused to travel without him, provisions had also been made for her to bring Dom with her to the ball.

When the offer had been made, Beth had almost wept with relief to accept. The nest-egg she'd thought would get her through the first year of Dom's life had been depleted far more quickly than she'd anticipated. She'd been at a real crossroads. She wasn't emotionally ready to put Dom in childcare and return to work but the bills were piling up and her rent, like everything else, had increased. She'd never been so skint in her life.

It was hard to believe that a little over a year ago the future had been so rosy. Beth had earned enough to rent a small flat but that had been all she'd needed. She'd been a single woman enjoying the London life with enough disposable income to eat out regularly, watch a live show or see a band whenever the mood struck. Her career had been going from strength to strength too but then tragedy had struck in a full-pronged attack and now she was in serious danger of losing the flat she loved so much and having to be put into social housing.

If it came to it, then she would cope. Dom's emotional welfare and wellbeing meant more than anything. The poor mite, orphaned by the time he'd turned three months, needed all the love and security she could give. Beth could never replace his mother but she hoped that, as he grew up, he would take her love and support for granted just as he would have taken Caroline's.

As an orphan herself, Beth knew how important and necessary this was.

She did not begrudge what she was doing for

Dom and refused to call it a sacrifice. What Caroline had done had been a sacrifice. She'd given her life so her child could live.

But, if her perilous finances weren't enough to contend with, there was also was the spectre of Alessio Palvetti hanging over her head.

Dom's powerful biological uncle had discovered Dom's existence and immediately thrown his weight about, emailing Beth from his ivory tower in Milan to demand access. Remembering the solemn promise she'd made to his parents to keep Dom far from Alessio and the other Palvettis for ever, she'd refused. Alessio had been undaunted and had got his expensive lawyers on the case, going as far as to offer her a million pounds in exchange for him taking custody of Dom. She had dismissed the offer out of hand and made it clear she would consider any further contact harassment and take appropriate action to protect Dom and herself against it.

She hadn't heard from him since but didn't believe his silence would last. He was too rich and too powerful to be held off for ever.

Beth loved Dom fiercely. She'd been present at his birth and there at his mother's death.

She would do anything to protect him, and if that meant fighting one of Europe's richest and most secretive families then so be it.

The money being offered to organise the masquerade ball was the life-saver she needed.

She hadn't seen Valente in the flesh since their initial meeting but as he was the liaison between Giannis and her they'd communicated daily with emails and video calls. What had started as purely professional communication had slowly transformed into something friendlier. Not only was he the sexiest man she'd ever met but he was easy to work with. He rarely questioned her judgement and, when he did, his points were valid and never cutting.

She'd found herself thinking about him a lot in the evenings when rocking Dom to sleep. And in the days when she was working on her laptop, co-ordinating things whilst simultaneously trying to keep Dom entertained. And at night…

Her skin suddenly heated to remember the dream she'd had of him. It had been a couple of weeks ago, long enough for the details to fade, but the hot, sticky feeling she'd woken with that night had stayed with her for a long time. For a few days after, she'd found it hard to meet his eye even though they'd been speaking via laptops.

He strode over to them, a head taller than everyone else in the vicinity, his lean body wrapped in dark trousers and an open-necked navy shirt that hugged his muscular chest, oblivious to the stares he received, a lazy smile playing on his lips.

When he reached them and extended a hand to her, the cuff of his sleeve pulled back with the motion to reveal a glimpse of fine, dark hair.

'Beth, it's good to see you again.' His thick Italian accent had a richness to it that made her think of strong coffee liqueur.

Her stomach tightened under the spotlight of his green eyes.

She'd forgotten how vivid they were in the flesh, the colour of emerald, contrasting sharply with the deep olive hue of his skin and the thick, black curls of his hair and dark, stubbled jaw. She knew women who would kill to have sweeping lashes as long and thick as his. Set in a chiselled face with a strong nose and firm mouth, he truly was heartbreakingly gorgeous.

Over the beats of a heart that had suddenly started a strangely rapid and erratic tempo, she reached out her hand and found her fingers enveloped in a firm shake that sent heat trickling through her.

She felt strangely breathless. 'You didn't say you would be meeting us.'

His eyes gleamed. 'My task this weekend is to assist you.'

Was she imagining the flirtatious tone and intensity of his stare…?

'Have the caterers arrived at the palace yet?' she asked as she removed her hand from his hold.

For all the friendliness that had developed between them through their communications, theirs was a professional relationship. Her dream had been exactly that. A dream. It didn't mean anything.

'They arrived as I was leaving. Everything is exactly as it should be. Your organisational skills are exceptional.'

Warmed by the compliment, she demurred. 'As you know very well, it was a team effort, and besides a six-week deadline to organise the masquerade ball of the century forces the mind to focus.'

Another gleam flashed before he peered down into the pram. He stared at Dom for what felt like an age before raising his gaze back to her. 'This is your son?'

The flirtatious sparkle that had been in his eyes had vanished. It didn't take a rocket scientist to figure out why—Valente had just remembered Beth was a mother...

Either that or she'd imagined the interest she'd seen in his eyes. The latter was most likely. Beth was seriously out of practice with the big, wide world and the flirtatious practices that went on in it. She'd never been party to the flirtatious practices when she'd been a full-time part of it.

'This is Dom,' she confirmed. Telling Valente she was Dom's legal guardian and not his biological mother would only lead to the inevitability of further questions. Caroline's death was still too raw for her to talk about it without turning into an emotional mess. The next twenty-four hours were going to be manically busy. She needed to focus on the job she was being paid to do. 'I would introduce you but he's only just gone off to sleep.'

He cast one more look at the sleeping baby. 'Let's get you to the palace and introduce you to the nanny who will look after him while you work.'

So saying, he picked up her suitcase as easily as if it were filled with nothing but air and carried it to the exit.

Keeping step with him, Beth found herself wondering, not for the first time, how a man who exuded such raw power as Valente could be comfortable working for anyone but himself. Even the way he composed his emails suggested a man who should be ordering minions around, not a man earning a living doing another's bidding.

When Alessio stepped out of the airport, he found the sun had risen in the Viennese morning sky. Its hazy beauty passed him by.

That was his orphaned nephew sleeping in the pram.

'Have you been to Vienna before?' he asked Beth. He needed to keep conversation flowing.

Until a few minutes ago, the closest he'd come

to Domenico, the child Beth called Dom, was through photographs.

His plan had worked seamlessly. Beth was here and she'd brought his nephew with her.

And she still had no idea who he really was.

There had been only a small chance Beth would recognise him. Alessio, like the rest of the Palvettis, guarded his privacy zealously and the few pictures of him in the public domain were obscured. There was nothing in the way of similarity between him and his deceased brother either, in personality or looks.

It had been tough, learning his brother had died in a drunken accident without a family reconciliation, tough to learn he'd secretly married and tough to learn how long he'd been dead. His brother's remains had been interred in a small cemetery in London rather than in his rightful place in the family plot in Milan. But to learn Domenico and his wife had given guardianship of their son to a stranger, a woman who was not even a blood relative on his mother's side…?

That had been the hardest blow.

Domenico's estrangement from and loathing of his family had gone beyond the grave. It had been the ultimate act of defiance against a family who had pandered to all his selfish needs and fanciful dreams.

Alessio had pushed his grief and fury towards his dead brother aside and set about bringing his nephew home. He would not allow the son to suffer for his father's petulance. Domenico's son was a Palvetti and deserved to be raised as such, not be left in the care of a stranger who didn't even share his blood.

Employing a private investigative team to dig into the guardian's life, he'd discovered she was a single twenty-four-year-old woman. Doubtless, she would be pleased to be rid of the burden of an orphaned child. Or so he'd thought.

He'd sent her a polite email requesting that they meet. She had replied with a curt 'No.' He'd got his lawyers involved but she'd remained unmoved. Assuming she was holding out for a financial offer from him—he'd learned the unpaid leave she'd taken from her workplace, presumably to care for his nephew, had left her dirt-poor—he'd offered her a million pounds for custody of his nephew.

Her instant dismissal of this offer and her threats to take legal action if he continued his 'harassment' had intrigued rather than angered him. By this point his investigators had compiled their final reports on her and what he'd learned had made interesting reading. Before going on leave, Beth had been a successful events manager.

A career-minded woman with a clear affection for his nephew…? A plan had germinated in his mind.

Alessio had wanted to spend a couple more years at the helm of Palvetti, the exclusive jewellery and perfumery business founded by his great-grandparents, before taking the ultimate step of selecting a wife and continuing the family dynasty. But if he was to take custody of his nephew that meant bringing his life plan forward. He would employ wraparound childcare, but his nephew would need a mother. Alessio's own mother had never been maternal but her feminine influence had been strong in his life and he wanted his nephew to have that same influence.

But marriage was not an institution to go into on a whim and investigative reports on a person only revealed so much. He needed to learn for himself if Beth was as ideal a candidate in real life as she was on paper.

That was when Alessio had contacted his old friend and called in the favour owed from their English school days. In return for Alessio providing an alibi that had saved Giannis Basinas from expulsion twenty years ago, Giannis would host a ball in the heart of Vienna, in the sumptuous palace he'd bought a few years ago and spent millions renovating. And he would employ White's Events to run it for him with the specific request that Beth Hardingstone be the manager for it.

Alessio's name would not be mentioned in the same breath as the masquerade ball. This was not only to keep Beth Hardingstone oblivious to his plans. Alessio lived his life quietly and discreetly, far from the media spotlight, keeping the Palvetti mystique that his great-grandparents had first cultivated and which enhanced the allure of their brand.

With no idea of the real reason for her being there, Beth answered his question with a cheery, 'I've always wanted to visit Vienna but this is the first job to bring me here.'

They'd reached his car, a gleaming black four-wheel drive. He clicked the fob to unlock it.

'Is this yours?' she asked with obvious surprise.

'It's for work.' Another evasion of the truth, he acknowledged ruefully as he opened the back door. Intrinsically honest, he found the deception about his identity increasingly hard to maintain.

Beth opened the back door then fixed large brown eyes as velvety as chocolate on him with a smile. 'You remembered a baby seat.'

He nodded. Damn, but she was beautiful when she smiled.

He'd been struck by that smile at their first meeting then in all their subsequent video calls. Her wide, generous mouth naturally turned upwards, as if smiling were her default position.

Today she'd dressed in a pair of slim-fitting cream trousers that rested above her ankles and a striped grey and white shirt. On her feet were flat ballerina-slipper-style shoes which, remembering the heels she'd worn to their first meeting, he guessed were for the practical reason of having a child in tow. Her long, dark hair had been left loose, the slight breeze lifting random silky strands, some falling across her pretty heart-shaped face. She wore no make-up that he could see but, with her lightly golden, clear complexion and those large, chocolaty eyes, she didn't need it.

She reached into the pram and unstrapped Dom.

Alessio held his breath as she carefully lifted the sleeping infant out.

The bundle in her arms was the reason he was doing all this. This bundle was a Palvetti, flesh of his flesh.

He cleared his throat. 'Do you need help?'

'I'm fine, thank you,' she replied with a cheerful smile, oblivious to the rush of blood pounding through him at this first clear sighting of his nephew.

With obvious practice, she placed the baby into the car seat then leaned over to fiddle with the straps to secure him.

Suddenly Alessio found his attention transfixed on her pert bottom.

His mouth dried and the blood rushing through him rapidly heated and diverted to concentrate in his loins.

It was a primitive reaction, the like of which he hadn't experienced since his teenage years.

'Aha!'

He blew out a puff of air and willed the burgeoning ache to subside. 'Sorry?'

She turned her head and wrinkled her nose. 'This was a bit more complicated than I thought it would be but I got there in the end.' Then she grinned again and turned back to Domenico to place a kiss on his cheek.

Pulling himself together, Alessio put her luggage in the boot of the car while Beth climbed into the front passenger seat. When he was done, and feeling more in control of his functions, he jumped into the driver's seat.

The moment he closed the door he found his senses springing back to life as a heady fragrance dived into him. Beth's perfume.

Dio, it was the most mouth-watering of scents.

'Ready?' He put the car into gear.

'Absolutely.' She laughed, an infectious, melodic tinkle. 'Take me to the palace!'

He grinned back.

Inappropriate though his responses were at this moment, he welcomed them.

Having worked with her these past six weeks, albeit remotely, he'd come to the conclusion that his initial thoughts had been correct. Beth would be an asset for any business.

Factor in her natural beauty, and his visceral response to her, and she had the exact traits he required in a wife.

CHAPTER TWO

BETH'S TIREDNESS HAD GONE. Now she buzzed with the adrenaline that always came when an event was within touching distance. She had never worked so hard in her life as she had these past six weeks. Lucinda, her boss, had diverted staff and resources to her, allowing Beth to coordinate everything with a military precision she hadn't known she was capable of.

She'd never got by on so little sleep, either. The hours during which Dom slept or napped had been spent ensuring everything Giannis Basinas required for his masquerade ball was exactly as it should be.

In only nine hours the guests would arrive. She had arranged events with impressive guest lists before but this one had made her gasp. Paying the extortionate sum to dance and be entertained were the world's most famous faces: European royalty, Hollywood royalty, billionaires, heirs and heiresses, artists… This was a ball guaranteed to make news.

She thought of the plans that must have been changed so high society could attend the masquerade ball at such short notice—the cancelled holidays, the rearranged schedules…

If it all went wrong it would be her neck on the chopping block.

But if it all went right then a healthy bonus would be hitting Beth's depleted bank account.

The salary she'd been paid for the ball up to this point had enabled her to pay her rent and buy Dom some new clothes. If she received the bonus she would have enough money to keep them going until her year's leave was up with enough spare for any future legal battle with Alessio Palvetti.

She would then have the difficult decision of whether or not to return to work.

'You've gone quiet,' Valente said, cutting through her thoughts. 'Is something on your mind?'

She cast him a quick glance. His attention was fixed on the clean, wide road before them. There was something incredibly reassuring about his command behind the wheel. Not once in their thirty-minute journey from the airport had she pressed an imaginary brake. 'I'm just thinking.'

'About what?'

She laughed. 'What do you think? The guests are due in nine hours. There's a lot that can go wrong in those nine hours.'

'Nothing is going to go wrong.'

'Speaks the voice of experience?'

'No, speaks the voice of someone who has found much to be impressed with your organisational talents.'

Embarrassed at how ridiculously flattered she felt at the compliment, she turned her face to look back out of the window. The view outside was almost as good as the view beside her. Little wonder this was a city famed for its romanticism. The architecture alone, grandeur and beauty at every turn of the head, was enough to make her catch her breath.

Sitting beside Valente kept making her catch her breath too. The longer she sat beside him, the more aware she became of his scent, the capable fingers controlling the steering wheel and the tensing of the strong thighs whenever he changed gear.

The longer she sat beside him, the more she became aware of *him*.

She cleared her throat and answered, 'The proof of the pudding's in the eating.'

'What does that mean?'

'That we won't know how good my organisational skills really are until the ball's over.'

'Why are you so nervous?'

'I've never undertaken an event of this magnitude before... Is that the palace?'

They'd turned into an enormous courtyard with a water fountain right in the centre of it. Surrounding the courtyard like a titanic curved horseshoe rose the most beautiful building she had ever seen.

Gleaming white under the rising sun, it was impossible to count the number of windows, all aligned with perfect symmetry over three high storeys, or count the ornate white pillars. Dozens and dozens and dozens of them.

No wonder it had quickly become famed as the most expensive hotel in Europe.

The same sense of awe enveloped her when, Dom in her arms, she climbed the wide, curved steps and stepped through the main doors.

She thought she knew every inch of the palace's ground floor from the photos, videos and scale drawings she'd been provided with but nothing could have prepared her for the reality.

If she closed her eyes, she could believe she was an eighteenth-century princess.

If she closed her eyes she could pretend not to be intensely aware of Valente watching her so closely.

'Let's get you to your suite,' he murmured. 'Dom's nanny is waiting for you.'

Pulling herself out of her stupor, she followed him through the richly decorated corridors and up a flight of stairs, as wide as her flat, covered in thick royal blue carpet. They took a left at the top and walked to the far end of the mezzanine to her designated room.

She gasped.

'This can't be for me.'

Valente had not been kidding when he'd called it a suite.

Dazzling green eyes fixed on her. 'You have a child. We weren't going to put you in the servants' quarters. Your outfit for the ball is hanging on your wardrobe.'

But she could see more than amusement in his gaze and that warm feeling trickled through her again, delving deep through her veins to coil into her bones and right into her core.

The glint in his eyes, the flare of his nostrils…

One of the many doors of the suite opened and a middle-aged woman appeared wearing a navy dress with a white sash tied around the waist.

Beth blinked and breathed a sigh of relief as she hurried over to introduce herself.

There was kindness in the nanny's eyes and Beth's nerves over handing Dom into the care of a stranger, however highly qualified and impeccable the references, evaporated.

'I need to check in with Giselle before we do anything else,' she told Valente when everything that could be discussed about Dom's care had been discussed and they were heading back to the ground floor.

Dom was going to be fine. The nanny would take good care of him.

Beth had a job to do and it was time to get going on it.

Giselle was the manager of the palace's hotel. While she had no involvement with the ball itself, many of the guests were staying there.

Valente pulled his car keys out of his pocket. 'I will leave you to it.'

'Are you going somewhere?' she asked, surprised.

His smile was faint but the gleam in his eyes was vivid. 'I have an appointment to attend but I will be back by noon. Call me if you need anything.'

And then he strode out of the palace, leaving her feeling something that smacked strangely of disappointment but which she pushed aside.

Beth did not mix business and pleasure. She never had and never would, not even for a man who made her heartbeat go into overdrive as Valente did.

Having committed the ground floor layout to memory, she found the manager's office easily and entered it, to find a severe-looking, diminutive blonde woman sat behind a huge desk.

'Giselle?' she asked.

The woman rose to her feet with a smile. 'Beth?'

She smiled back. 'Lovely to finally meet you in person. Any problems since we last spoke?'

'None. Any problems your end?'

'Not that I know of. Valente said the caterers have arrived...'

'Who?'

'Valente Cortada. I've been reporting to him for the ball.'

'I have never heard this name.'

'Oh.' Flummoxed, Beth thought hard, trying to remember if Valente had said he actually worked at the hotel. 'He must work for Mr Basinas directly.'

'That must be it because he does not work here. And, yes, the caterers have arrived. I will take you to them shortly. Can I offer you refreshment before we get started?'

Beth put her professional head on and got down to business.

But, as the busy hours passed, the disquiet she'd felt at Giselle's unfamiliarity to Valente's name stayed with her.

Alessio locked the documents his lawyer had given him during their meeting in his suite's safe and called his PA in Milan to check in.

He disliked being away from the business. For his entire life he'd known that, if he worked hard enough, one day Palvetti would be under his control. It might be the family business but it had not been handed to him on a plate. He'd had to prove himself. The top job gave ultimate control of the business and a majority share. If the natural heir was deemed unfit for the job, the role would be passed to another family member better qualified. In Palvetti, there was a role to suit everyone's skills and inclinations. It was and always had been a family business.

Alessio had coveted the top job from as far back as he could remember. School holidays had been spent shadowing various family members in their differing roles. When he'd graduated from university with a first-class economics and management degree, he'd started work for Palvetti immediately, reporting directly to his father.

At that time there had been something of a sales slump that had hit their profit margins. Alessio's suggestions to turn the slump around had been implemented and within three years profits had risen by nine per cent. When his father had retired shortly after Alessio's thirtieth birthday, the family board had been unanimous—the top job was Alessio's. Under his guidance, Palvetti had gone from strength to strength. Their target of breaking into the crucial Chinese market had been a resounding success. Their jewellery graced the necks, wrists, ears and fingers of the world's richest people and their luxury scents soaked their skin.

Palvetti was enjoying a boom and Alessio had no intention of allowing that boom to turn into a bust. He would not risk taking his eye off the ball.

His brother had not had the same sense of duty or destiny. Despite Alessio's and his parents' best efforts, Domenico had shown nothing but contempt for the business.

Domenico had refused to embrace anything but his own selfish pleasures.

Judging by the coroner's report into his death, the years of estrangement had only made him worse.

What reckless selfishness had spurred him to ride his bicycle on London's busy roads with enough alcohol in his bloodstream to defrost a freezer when he had a six months' pregnant wife at home waiting for him?

Had his brother *wanted* to die? He'd written his will only weeks before his death.

What kind of character would his nephew

have? Alessio ruminated as he searched for Beth. Would he take after his father or would Alessio's influence be enough to steer him on the right path?

The great ballroom was a bustle of activity, dozens of people working together and separately to transform the room into a magical wonderland. Supervising it all was Beth, clipboard and tablet in hand, standing at the base of the stage the orchestra would be performing on, chatting to a couple of the workers.

He admired the sense of calm she exuded. The nerves she'd displayed in his car were either gone or she'd hidden them. She had the perfect leadership traits: calmness and competence. If a leader was prone to panic, it infected the workers.

About to approach her, his phone vibrated in his pocket. As he answered it, her gaze suddenly found him.

Something he could not explain passed between them in the look they shared in that moment, something that made all the cells in his body thicken.

There had to be thirty feet between them but

his body reacted to her stare as if she were right in front of him.

He inhaled and raised a hand in greeting.

Her lips curved into a half-smile. She waved her fingers.

She stepped in his direction but had moved only a couple of paces when another worker hurried over to her.

She said something then looked back at Alessio.

He gestured that he needed to go.

She nodded and smiled again before giving the worker her full attention.

Alessio left the ballroom to continue his phone conversation but with the thrill of anticipation racing through his veins.

'Valente?' Beth said when he answered her call.

'Is something the matter?'

A not unpleasant shiver raced up her spine as the richness of his voice seeped through her ear and burrowed deep inside her.

'There's been a mix-up with my uniform. The outfit left in my suite is a ball gown. I've spoken to Giselle but she doesn't know anything about it.'

In the main bedroom of her suite she'd found her uniform hanging on the wardrobe as Valente had told her it would be, covered in grey wrapping with the palace insignia and her name tied to the hanger. Beth, like all the other White's Events staff and palace staff working at the ball that night, had provided her vital statistics for her outfit. Expecting the same black uniform everyone else had been given, she'd been gobsmacked when she'd removed the cover to find an obviously expensive strapless, floor-length gold ball gown.

'There is no mix-up. That's your uniform for the evening.'

'A ball gown? I need a proper uniform to wear so that guests and staff can identify me...'

His laughter rumbled through her skin. 'I am afraid it is too late to change it, *bella*. Enjoy it—consider it a reward for all your hard work. I will see you shortly.'

Before she could protest any further he ended the call.

She sighed and fingered the hem of the dress. It felt like silk. Further examination of it revealed no label to identify its maker.

The dress was incredible. But it was not an

appropriate dress for her to wear that night. As the event manager she needed to be easily identifiable, not look as if she could pass as one of the guests.

But, as Valente had so helpfully pointed out, it was too late to change it. She had only a two-hour window until the first guests arrived.

Instead of getting ready, she took Dom from Miranda, the nanny, gave him his bottle and played with him for a while. She wished she didn't have to leave him again that night. Miranda had been great in sending her regular updates on his welfare that day but, despite being so busy, Beth had missed him horrendously. He'd been at her side since his birth.

She kissed his plump cheek then kissed his button nose. 'Mummy needs to get ready now,' she told him, before handing him back to Miranda.

Calling herself 'Mummy' was something that still caused a wrench in her heart. Caroline was his mummy but Caroline had made Beth promise to *be* his mummy. It was a promise she would keep for the rest of her life.

Beth showered quickly, dried her hair and

applied a little make-up then, with Miranda's help, got into the dress.

It fitted perfectly. The box that had lain on the floor beneath it contained a pair of gold shoes that also fitted perfectly.

Who, she wondered moodily, had authorised such a dress for her? Giannis Basinas? If him, then why? She still hadn't met him, all communication having been done through Valente.

Had *Valente* authorised the dress?

Which begged the question of who Valente was to Giannis. Her assumption that he worked at the hotel had proved to be wrong.

But there was no time to wonder any longer. The guests would start arriving soon. She needed to be in the ballroom. She might be dressed like a princess but she was at this ball to work.

Work or not, there was no denying that the anticipation running through her was on a scale she felt right down to her toes.

Alessio entered the already crowded reception room and helped himself to a glass of champagne. Being a good head taller than most people gave him the advantage of seeing over the elaborately dressed, highly excited guests, and the pianist entertaining them, but he couldn't see Beth.

He cut through the crowd. At the ballroom entrance he nodded at the security man guarding it, who opened the door for him.

And there she was, clipboard and tablet in hand as they'd been earlier, making her way around the tables lining the east and west walls of the room, double checking that everything was perfect…

His throat closed as he took in the perfection of *her*.

The dress he'd selected for her fitted as if the seamstress had sewn it with Beth as her mannequin. The curves of her body, that the outfits in which he'd seen her before had only hinted at, were more feminine than he'd imagined. She'd swept her dark hair into an elegant chignon which exposed the grace of her neck and emphasised the beauty of her bone structure.

If his plan continued its successful path, it would not be long before his lips grazed that graceful neck…and the rest of that ravishing body.

Beth had beauty and an exquisite eye for detail. With his guidance, she had the potential to be as great an asset to Palvetti as all the other Palvetti spouses had been.

With his guidance, she would become the perfect Palvetti wife.

He just had to keep the deception going a little longer, until the ball was over. He imagined there would be a scene when she discovered who he really was and he wanted that scene to be conducted in private.

He finished his champagne and walked to her. 'Good evening, *bella*,' he said.

She smiled to see him before her eyes narrowed a touch. 'Hi, Valente... I see you've been given a non-uniform to wear too.'

'My non-uniform does not look as good as yours,' he replied evasively. His non-uniform had been hand-stitched by Milan's finest tailor. 'You look beautiful.'

Her lightly golden cheeks flushed with colour and her lips pulled in before she said, 'That's kind of you to say. So, what do you think? Does the ballroom match Mr Basinas's expectations?'

He slowly turned around to take in everything anew and nodded.

Gold, silver and white balloons hung from the high grand ceiling, matching heavy drapes lining the walls. The tables followed the same theme; ornately decorated and with centrepieces topped with feathers and miniature gold masks. The orchestra was on the stage, the musicians tuning their instruments, the champagne fountain already flowing.

'Have you seen the other rooms?' she asked.

'I haven't seen them finished. Show me.'

She led the way, taking him through myriad other rooms adorned with the same decorations: the dining room, where a hot and cold buffet would be served throughout the night, and where a string quartet was tuning their instruments to entertain the diners; the cocktail lounge, filled with sofas and armchairs for those who wanted to catch their breath and listen to the music of a lounge pianist; the chocolate room, filled with edible creations hand-made in Switzerland and the disco room, which wouldn't be opened until after the midnight fireworks, and would no doubt be filled with younger revellers wanting a break from waltzing to let their hair down to more familiar songs.

It was hard to believe this had all been achieved in only six weeks.

'You have done an incredible job,' he told her as they walked back to the ballroom.

'I can't take the credit. It was a team effort, as you very well know.' Beth would not allow her team's achievements to be diminished. Eight members of her team had been camped in the palace for the past three weeks beavering away.

'You directed it all. You pulled it together. This is your vision. Accept the plaudits and be proud of what you've achieved.'

'I haven't achieved anything yet,' she reminded him. 'As I said this morning, the proof of the pudding's in the eating. Let's wait to hear Mr Basinas's and the guests' feedback before getting carried away.'

He opened his mouth but whatever he was about to say was cut off by the master of ceremonies approaching them.

'Five minutes,' he informed her gravely.

Her stomach knotted. For a moment she feared she would be sick.

Five minutes?

'Excuse me,' she murmured to Valente. 'I need to get in position.'

He cast her a look that made her belly melt.

Her bones had melted just looking at him. She had not thought he could be more handsome but tonight, freshly shaved and dressed in a deep maroon, long-tailed dinner jacket the men had all been instructed to wear—colour and style optional—with matching trousers, black shirt and black bow-tie, he looked devastating.

She hurried back into the ballroom to take her position by the champagne fountain. Moments later the orchestra played its first beat, the ballroom doors opened and the master of ceremonies formally announced the ball open.

CHAPTER THREE

THE GUESTS POURING into the ballroom made a spectacular sight. The dress code was formal, but with an invitation to be colourful, and the guests had taken it at its word. Dresses every colour of the spectrum were there, the ladies resembling creatures from a fairy tale of long ago, the men dashing in their rich long-tails. The masks, all hand-crafted, ranged from simple yet hauntingly beautiful pieces that covered only the eyes to elaborate, bejewelled face-covering creations. It was a sight that made Beth's heart soar.

As the guests lined the sides of the great ballroom, ladies to the left, gentlemen to the right, a quartet of ballet dancers from Compania de Ballet de Casillas performed a short opening dance to welcome them, before gracefully leaving and being replaced by two-dozen professional ballroom dancers.

The professionals danced the first waltz alone

and then the master of ceremonies instructed the gentlemen to choose a partner. Soon, four hundred people filled the floor, the dresses whirling in a wonderful kaleidoscope of colour.

For the next dance, the ladies got to choose their partner. Only one man refused to relinquish his dance partner, and as that man was Giannis Basinas himself no one was going to argue the point with him.

From that moment, the evening passed in a blur, and Beth found herself able to breathe properly.

She regularly monitored the other rooms, unobtrusively checking and double-checking everything, ready to instruct a team member to fix the tiniest imperfection.

She had lost track of time when she made another return to the ballroom and received a tap on the shoulder.

Spinning around, expecting to find a male guest requesting a dance—something she had had to decline four times already—her heart leapt into her throat to find Valente standing before her, two flutes of champagne in his hands.

He held one out to her and bowed his head. 'For you, my lady.'

Much as she would have liked to pretend otherwise, Beth had been alert to his presence the entire evening. Every small glimpse had set her pulses thumping.

She blinked away the effect of his emerald eyes boring into her and the drumming effect playing in her head, echoes from her thundering heart. 'That's kind, but I don't drink when I'm working.'

'You are officially off the clock as of now.'

She rolled her eyes and strove to keep her voice light-hearted. 'I'll be off the clock at four in the morning when the ball finishes.'

'I have spoken to Giannis. He is exceptionally pleased with how well everything is going. Now is the time for you to turn your work head off and enjoy yourself.'

'Is that what you've been doing?' she asked. 'Enjoying yourself? Because I haven't seen you do anything that looks like work.'

'Dance with me and I'll tell you all about it.'

'Valente, I'm working. I can't dance.'

'I told you, you are officially off the clock. Your work is done. Your assistant can take charge. Your instructions now are to enjoy yourself.'

'Is that an official order?'

'Assolutamente.' A wicked gleam flashed in his eyes that made her belly melt all over again. 'And the first official order for enjoying yourself is to drink this glass of champagne. The second is to dance with me.'

Valente was the intermediary between Beth and Giannis. He spoke for the Greek billionaire. If he said she was off duty then it had to be true.

Romance filled the air within the palace. The thought of joining the happy revellers on the dance floor with the most handsome man there was far more appealing than it should be.

When he offered the champagne to her a second time, she took it from him and brought the flute to her lips. The bubbles exploded in her mouth. 'If you're lying to me and I get a rollicking for skiving off, you can pay the bonus I'll forfeit.'

'You will not forfeit the bonus.'

He sounded so confident in this assertion that Beth relaxed enough to laugh.

Lines appeared on his handsome face as he grinned, the only imperfections on a face that could have been designed by a renaissance master. And the lines weren't even imperfections, serving to enhance the gorgeous face she could not help herself from drinking in.

He held his flute to hers.

She chinked hers to it. In unison, they drank.

Valente placed the empty flutes on the tray of a passing waiter then held his hand out to her. 'Time to dance.'

But still she hesitated.

She wanted to dance with him. She wanted it more than she should. And that was the cause of her hesitation.

What if he wanted more than just a dance?

And why did that thought make her skin tingle as if a thousand electric ants were zipping through her veins?

Through the years Beth had been asked to dance by countless numbers of men. Valente was the first man she had wanted to say yes to.

She reminded herself about all the event staff she'd seen through the years involve themselves with rich clients or the client's staff or guests. When alcohol flowed freely, inhibitions loosened and hedonistic pleasure became the aim. She would not be like the poor events staff she'd observed through the years fall for the practised patter, kidding themselves that the attention was anything more than an eye for the chance of a willing body for a night's pleasure, discarded and forgotten when the sun came up.

Beth had come to distrust rich, powerful men. In her experience, they were the worst for treating women as commodities.

Domenico had been the only rich man she'd met who hadn't treated women like that. He'd loved Caroline and had treated her with the utmost respect.

But Domenico had forfeited his riches out of loathing for his rich, powerful family. He'd preferred to be poor and happy than rich and cruel like his brother, Alessio. His stories about what went on behind the closed doors of the rich and powerful had only hardened Beth's distrust of the elite.

Valente was not a rich man. The power he exuded was a figment of her imagination.

The dance had finished, the guests pairing off again for the next one.

'Enough stalling,' he scolded. He took the matter out of her control by taking hold of her hand and marching her to the dance floor.

'I really can't dance,' she warned, laughing,

although unable to understand *why* she was laughing.

What harm would one dance do? It wasn't as if she were agreeing to marry him!

He guided her to possibly the only empty space on the floor. 'It is easy. I will teach you.'

'You can dance?'

'*Si*. Follow my lead and you will be fine.' He bowed. 'Now you must curtsey.'

Laughing again, she curtsied then allowed him to take her right hand in his left.

She took a quick peek at where the other women were placing their left hands and placed hers on Valente's bicep. It was rock-hard.

The laughter died in her throat when he slipped his right hand around her waist and pulled her to him. Her nose was level with his neck. The scent of his cologne coiled through her and something else, something like warm treacle, pooled low in her abdomen and with it came a flash of the dream she'd had of him, of them…

Slowly she raised her head to meet his eyes. The amusement that had been in the emerald gaze just moments ago had died.

After a long, silent beat passed between them,

the faintest of smiles curved his lips. Her own lips tingled and she felt a sudden yearn to press them to his, a yearn that dissolved when the first note of the music rang out and suddenly she was being spun around the room in the most heavenly of arms.

For such a tall, muscular man, Valente danced with an elegance that made her dazed mind think he'd done this many times. His assured grace and utter control allowed her to relax into the dance and, as he spun her around the great ballroom, weaving seamlessly between the other dancing couples, she imagined herself as a princess from days gone by waltzing in the arms of her very own Prince Charming.

When the dance ended, Alessio kept tight hold of her. 'One more,' he murmured into her ear.

The rays from her answering smile beamed straight into his loins.

Impulse had driven him to ask her to dance. He'd spent the evening observing her, the desire to have her in his arms growing with every passing minute.

The compulsory ballroom dancing lessons

he'd endured at his English boarding school were finally paying off.

'Where did you learn to dance?' she asked when they were on their third waltz, one set at a slower tempo.

'As a child.' Soon there would be no more need for evasion.

Her head tilted as she studied him. 'What is it you do for Giannis Basinas?'

'Why do you ask?'

'None of the hotel staff have heard of you.' There was no accusation in the beautiful chocolate eyes, just a soft curiosity.

He pulled her a little closer. Their bodies were almost touching. She didn't pull back. 'Let's just say I have known Giannis for many years.'

'Is that all you will tell me?'

'For now.'

A spark flared in her eyes. Its brilliance flashed through him. 'Intriguing.'

He laughed but it was from discomfort rather than humour. Alessio knew this was the moment he should whisk her away somewhere private and tell her the truth, somewhere where they wouldn't be overheard.

Forget waiting until the morning. He had

waited long enough. Beth had passed every test he'd given her.

But he wanted to hold her in his arms for a few more dances first and savour the heady, erotic feeling flowing through his loins a little longer before the dilated softness flowing from her gaze turned into loathing.

The loathing wouldn't last long, he was sure. Beth was too practical to be dictated to by emotions.

The dance ended without any further conversation, and the master of ceremonies took to the stage to announce that there would be a short break from the dancing for the fireworks display being held in the grounds.

'Shall we?' He held his arm out to her.

She smiled, nodded and tucked her hand through it.

They followed the crowd through the ground floor of the palace to the famed gardens. Alessio had only taken a few breaths of the warm night air when there was a tap on his shoulder.

He turned and inwardly cringed to find Richard, an old university friend, standing there.

'Alessio Palvetti as I live and breathe!' Richard roared, obviously steaming drunk. 'How wonderful to see you! My God, man, how many years has it been?'

Not enough.

He felt Beth go rigid beside him.

'Hello, Richard,' he answered tightly.

'I thought it was you,' Richard shouted. 'I said to my wife, look, there's Alessio Palvetti. I must introduce you to her. She never believes me when I tell her we were at Oxford together.'

Richard's words washed over him.

He met Beth's frozen gaze. Her eyes were stark and wide. Slowly she extricated her hand from his arm and stepped back to wrap her arms tightly around her chest.

Alessio held her stare.

The first firework exploded in the sky.

Beth blinked then, turning as fast as the shooting rocket hurtling above them, fled.

Beth pushed her way through the crowd still spilling out into the gardens, the curses thrown at her as champagne was spilt in her wake nothing but a distant sound, the industrial fireworks showering the sky with luminescence melding with the drum beats exploding in her head.

Her lungs had cramped, fear fisting tightly in her stomach.

Back under the palace roof, she ran as fast as her heeled feet would carry her until she entered an unfamiliar room and spun around in panic.

She'd lost her bearings.

She covered her mouth with a shaking hand and forced herself to think. She had pored over the map of the palace for so many hours she knew it intimately but her brain had turned into stunned goo.

Think!

Instinct had her race to the door to the right of the room but it only led to another unfamiliar room.

Her instincts clearly weren't worth anything. If they had been, she would have had an inkling that Valente wasn't…was…

Oh, dear God, it had all been a lie.

Get to Dom.

She turned back and ran to the door to the left.

The palace's proportions that she had found so awe-inspiring on her arrival had become a frightening warren. The richly decorated walls had gained faces, the masks on the few guests who'd stayed inside rather than watch the fireworks coming to life to laugh at her.

That feeling, that the whole palace was laughing cruelly at her naivety, was compounded when she finally found the stairs and tripped on the third step. One of her shoes fell off. She stumbled on, pausing only to remove her remaining shoe, climbing the stairs as fast as she could but somehow feeling as if time itself had slowed and that she was ascending a mountain that was fighting back, a lucid, waking nightmare.

The nightmare showed no sign of letting up when she finally reached the door to her suite. She'd left her bag in the staff room. Her door key was in it.

The door was locked.

She banged on it and kept on banging until it was opened by the nanny.

'Where's Dom?' she gasped, uncaring of Miranda's blatant disapproval at this loud disruption.

Was she even a real nanny or a stooge set up by Valente… Alessio?

'Asleep.'

'He's here?'

'*Yes*. He's in his cot.'

But the nanny's word was not enough. Beth needed to see him with her own two eyes.

Dragging her jelly legs to the bedroom Dom had been appointed to share with the nanny, she pushed the door open.

The only illumination in the room came from the opened door. The cot was at the far wall. Beth crept over to it, her heart thundering, terrified that she would find it empty…

Dom lay in it on his back, tiny hands in fists either side of his head, sleeping peacefully, as snug as a bug in a rug.

The relief that surged through Beth to find him there safe and sound was so great that she doubled over and gulped air into her burning lungs.

But the relief was only temporary. Danger remained close. Remembering the fury on Alessio's face when that man had called him by his real name, she figured his plans to snatch Dom from her had been interrupted.

Alessio's minions might be on their way right now to get him.

She had to take Dom *now*, and leave this palace before...

A large shadow filled the open doorway.

'No!' The word shot from her mouth as a howl and she straightened clumsily to spread her arms wide across the cot. If he wanted to get to Dom, he would have to get through her first.

Dom stirred, a tiny mewing sound coming from his cot.

Beth held her breath. She didn't dare take her eyes off Alessio, who remained at the threshold of the room.

'I'm sorry you had to discover the truth like that.' His words echoed off the walls.

Nausea roiled violently in her stomach. 'Sorry that it prevented you taking Dom, *Alessio*?'

She tried to keep a lid on the fresh panic gripping her as she took in the lean yet muscular proportions of the man with a new ominous perspective. If it came to a fight, she would never win.

But she would try. She would fight. She would do whatever it took to keep Dom out of the clutches of the man from whom she had sworn to protect him. She would protect her ward with her life.

He shook his head slowly. 'If I wanted to take him, I would have done so already.'

'Stay back!' He'd stepped into the room. The shoe she'd lost on the stairs was in his hand. 'Don't come any closer.'

She tensed her body, readying herself for the first physical fight of her life.

He took another step forward and placed the shoe on the dressing table.

Dom let out a loud cry.

Not wanting to take her eyes away from the slowly nearing Italian, she twisted an arm into the cot and groped carefully until she found Dom's belly and gently stroked it. He cried out again. It was a cry of pain.

Valente... Alessio...stopped walking.

He expelled a deep breath then stepped back to the door. At the threshold he called out, 'Miranda.'

The nanny appeared.

'I'm going to take Miss Hardingstone to my suite. Domenico needs attending to.'

'No!' But Dom's cries of pain were increasing and Beth could no longer bear the agony

in her heart to hear them. She turned quickly and scooped him into her arms. Immediately his cries lessened.

Holding him securely and rocking him gently, she turned to her adversary and fought unsuccessfully to hold her own tears back. 'Please, I am begging you, don't do this. Don't take him from me.'

CHAPTER FOUR

'BETH...' ALESSIO'S FACE contorted briefly before he took five long strides to her.

She shrank back, her bottom wedged against the cot.

He gazed down at her but made no attempt to remove the fractious baby from her arms. His voice was surprisingly gentle as he said, 'Listen to me, no one is taking Domenico from you, but we need to talk and it will be better if we can do that with privacy. My suite adjoins yours. Let Miranda take care of him and, when we're done talking, you can come back to him.'

Alessio watched Beth's face scrunch and her chest rise and fall rapidly, all the while rocking the baby in her arms.

He could curse.

He'd been prepared for screams, shouts and curses. He had not expected or been prepared for such anguish.

'Give Domenico to Miranda. You have my

word that you can return to him when we're done talking.'

She turned her pleading gaze to Miranda, who came to her side and carefully lifted Domenico from her arms.

'I'm not going anywhere,' the nanny murmured.

Beth nodded bravely before placing a tender kiss on the baby's forehead. 'Have you given him any of his infant painkiller?'

'He can have some more in half an hour. Don't worry. I'll look after him, I promise.'

She stepped away from them and rubbed her hands on her arms.

Knowing Beth would follow, Alessio walked to the door that adjoined their suites and unlocked it. Once in his own suite, he headed straight to the bar in the main lounge area and poured them both a hefty measure of single malt.

He held one out to her. 'Take it. You've had a shock. It will help.'

Chocolate eyes, red and puffy from crying, held his briefly before she took the glass from him and carried it to one of the sofas. Only when she had sat down did she take a large drink from it.

He watched her carefully as she fixed her gaze to the ceiling and held tightly to her glass.

Lowering himself onto an armchair, he said, 'I am sorry you had to find out the way you did. I was going to come clean in the morning.'

She turned her head and cast eyes swimming with anguish on him. 'You're really Alessio Palvetti?'

'Yes.'

Her head dropped forward. The silky hair that had been wound so elegantly was in disarray, brunette locks spilling out in all directions. 'This ball… How…? How did you do it?'

'Giannis and I have been friends since our school days. I asked him to host the ball in his palace and employ your company to run it. He owed me a favour and agreed.'

She rubbed the back of her neck and muttered, 'Must have been some favour.'

Beth thought of the astronomical sum of money that had been spent on the ball, not a cent of which had been recouped from the tickets. All the money raised through the four hundred guests who had each paid forty thousand euros to attend was going to charity. 'All this… just so you could get Dom?'

And, now he had Dom in his clutches, she had little doubt he'd taken the necessary precautions needed to stop Dom and her leaving the palace without him. He'd even put them into adjoining suites!

The lengths he'd gone to get them here proved him a master tactician who always thought a dozen moves ahead.

The rich were in a league of their own when it came to getting what they wanted. When money was no object, then any scruples or morality be damned. Alessio had been born without either.

'Do not misunderstand me. Getting custody of Domenico is my primary motivation. He is a Palvetti and he deserves to take his place with us, his family. In my care he can have everything but, if custody were all I wanted, he would already be with me.'

She took another sip of her drink. Normally she hated whisky in any of its forms but right then the burn it made in her throat was welcome. It was the fire she needed to cut through her despair. 'Then what *do* you want? I think of all the work we've done, all the hours spent, all the money spent—'

'I wanted to get to know you.'

She finally allowed herself to look at him. *'Why?'*

The emerald eyes that had turned her veins to treacle lasered into hers. He leaned forward and spoke quietly. 'I wanted to learn about you through more than the reports and photographs my investigators provided me with.'

'You had me investigated?'

'I thought it prudent to look into the character of the person caring for my nephew.'

Her head span so violently she felt dizzy with the motion.

He'd been spying on her.

She should have known Alessio's silence since she'd refused his offer of money in exchange for Dom had been ominous. She'd lulled herself into a false sense of security and underestimated him, and underestimated the lengths he would be prepared to go to.

Everything Domenico had said about his brother was true, and more.

Through the ringing in her ears, he continued. 'Do not worry. Any childhood indiscretions are your own concern. I only wanted to know about the last five years of your life, and what I learned about you intrigued me. It was clear to me from the investigator's reports and your refusal of my financial offer that you had an affection for my nephew.'

'Affection does not cover a fraction of the love I feel for him,' she told him fiercely.

'I am beginning to understand that for myself.'

'Good, because I will never let him go without a fight.'

'I understand that too but you must know that, if it came to a fight, you would never win. I could have gone through the British courts and made my case for custody—I think we are both aware that my wealth and power would have outmatched your efforts—but Domenico is familiar with you and it is better for him if you remain in his life than be cut off.'

She held his gaze and lifted her chin. 'I'm all he knows.'

He raised a nonchalant shoulder. 'But he is very young. If it comes to it, he will adapt without you quickly. For the avoidance of doubt, I do not want that outcome.'

'What outcome *do* you want?'

'Marriage.'

Drum beats joined the chorus of sound in her head. 'What on *earth* are you talking about?'

He rose from his seat and headed back to the bar. 'Once I have Domenico in Milan, it will be a simple matter for me to take legal guardianship of him.' He poured himself another large measure and swirled it in his glass. 'I recognise your genuine affection for each other and have no wish to separate you. In all our best interests, I am prepared to marry you.'

Dumbfounded, Beth shook her head, desperately trying to rid herself of all the noise in her ears so she could think properly. 'I wouldn't marry you if you paid me.'

He took a large swallow of his drink and stared at her with that same expressionless look. 'Then I take Domenico home and find another woman to marry and be a mother for him.'

She pinched her nose and breathed deeply. She would rather die than allow another woman to raise the little boy she loved so much.

But this was no bluff. She did not doubt that for a second.

'I would prefer not to take that option.' His words swam through the noise in her head she still couldn't drown out. 'But bringing Domenico home means the time is right for me to take a wife. He will thrive better if he has a permanent female influence in his life. A marriage between us is the ideal outcome for all of us and has the potential to be successful.'

'You're on a different planet if you believe that.'

'I do believe that.' The glimmer of a smile played on his lips. 'Palvetti is a family business and any woman I choose to marry will be a part of it. It's the reason I went to these lengths—I needed to be sure you were right for me and right for the business. I wanted to see how you worked under pressure in a business environment. I kept my identity a secret because I wanted you to get to know me without the poison I assumed my brother had fed you about me clouding your judgement. You have impressed me with your attention to detail and the way you handle your staff. These six weeks have shown we work well together, which is an essential component for any marriage I undertake.'

She could hardly credit what she was hearing. 'You would expect me to work for you?'

'Palvetti spouses are business partners. They are chosen with great care for that very reason.'

'Family dinners must be a great laugh,' she muttered sarcastically.

'We know how to have fun but the business always comes first.'

Her mind stretched back to remember Domenico having said, many times, that the family business came first in everything. There was no balance between work and home life. His mother had returned to work within a week of giving birth to him.

This, in a nutshell, was everything he had despised about his family and everything he had vowed to protect his own children against.

'We protect it for the next generation,' Alessio explained. 'If you marry me you will be a part of it, and tasked with protecting it for Domenico and any siblings and cousins he has. We will find a role suitable for your skills.'

The ringing in her ears returned with a vengeance.

'Siblings?' she queried faintly.

'At some point in the future, yes.' His eyes

held hers, emeralds glittering. 'If you marry me, be in no doubt ours will be a real marriage.'

The meaning in his voice was unambiguous.

Heat crawled all over her, firing through her bones and flaming her cheeks.

If she married him she would have to share his bed. She would have to sleep with him.

She tried to drag air into her closed lungs.

Marriage? To Alessio Palvetti, the man propped against the bar staring so intently at her she could feel the burn of his gaze on her skin…?

She dropped her eyes from his and tried to focus her attention on the plush carpet.

'This is a lot for me to take in,' she whispered when she could get her airways working again.

'I appreciate that but I think it is best to lay all the cards on the table. I don't want you to be under any illusions.'

'How nice of you after six weeks of blatant lies.'

'Only my identity was a lie. Everything else was real. Our rapport was real. The attraction was real…'

She shook her head violently and wrapped her arms tightly across her stomach. She didn't want to remember how her heart had thudded whenever she'd caught a glimpse of him or how her blood had turned to warmed treacle.

'Beth, look at me.' The tone in his voice demanded to be obeyed and her head lifted before her brain could stop it.

She met the hard stare and felt her heart thud tremulously all over again.

He gazed back at her for a moment that seemed to hang over them before his features softened slightly. 'The attraction was there from the start—you cannot deny that. We both felt it. There is desire between us and all the other ingredients needed for a successful marriage.'

Had it only been an hour ago that he had spun her around the dance floor?

She had felt like a princess in his arms. Her body had delighted to be held against him, had strained towards him.

Her lips still tingled in anticipation of a kiss that had never come.

That he could speak of the attraction in such a matter-of-fact way cut through her. He had played her in so many different ways but this one cut the deepest.

The man who had stolen into her dreams had

been the man from whom she had sworn to protect her ward.

How could she ever forgive herself?

'I gave you the chance to prove yourself to me and you exceeded my expectations,' he said into the silence. 'I could have taken Domenico at any point today. Instead I am giving you the opportunity to be a permanent part of his life.'

She felt as if she could cry all over again at the wretchedness of it all. 'How can you call it an opportunity when *I'm* his legal guardian?' But she knew he could overcome that legality in a heartbeat, especially now that he had her out of her home country. 'Don't your brother and sister-in-law's wishes and feelings count for anything?'

There was the barest flicker of a pulse in his jaw. 'I am respecting their wishes by making this offer to you. If he had lived, my brother would have returned to the fold, because he would have seen it was in Domenico's best interests. He died a poor man. Neither he nor his wife made financial provision for their son and you have suffered for it. Domenico is a Palvetti, and he deserves to be raised as one, and enjoy the wealth and privilege that's his by right.'

'Your brother would never have come back to the family fold,' she whispered. 'He despised the lot of you.'

'I wish I could say my opinions on him were any different.' He tipped the remaining Scotch down his throat. 'My brother was a leech but I will not allow his son to suffer for the mistakes his father made. Domenico is a Palvetti heir. If he has the aptitude, one day he will run the business as I do. He will not live in poverty and if you accept my proposal you can be saved from it too.'

'I don't need to be saved,' she retorted. 'I've always supported myself.'

His cynically raised brow at this assertion infuriated her. He'd had an investigator dig into her life and now thought he was an expert on her?

If he'd dug that little bit further into her history, he would know she'd had no choice but to support herself.

Beth had no family to go cap-in-hand to if times got hard. Her foster parents had been good people, and had kept her under their roof far longer than most foster placements, but she'd always known that the moment she turned eighteen she would be on her own.

Other than Caroline, she'd never had anyone to fall back on and now, with Caroline's death, her only emotional crutch had gone.

'I'm only skint at the moment because I've been on unpaid leave for eleven months. I'm perfectly capable of supporting Dom and myself.'

'In my care, Domenico will be more than supported—he will have the best of everything. You can have that too. All you have to do is say yes.' Expectation now gleamed in his eyes.

Desperation tore at her throat. 'You can't honestly expect me to give you an answer right now? I need time—'

'If your feelings for Domenico run as deep as you say they do then what do you need to think about? Do you want to be a continuing influence in his life or not? Everything is out in the open between us, and in the morning I shall return to Milan with Domenico. You need to decide, now, if you're going to be with us.'

Beth settled Dom in his carry-cot and, limbs and heart heavy, sat on the sofa in her suite.

While she waited for the knock on the door that would signal their departure from the palace, she switched her phone on and messaged her boss Lucinda to let her know she wouldn't be flying back with the rest of the White's Events staff. She couldn't bring herself to speak to her. She felt too sick to talk to anyone. The most she'd got her vocal cords to do since she'd given up on sleep was hum to Dom when she'd given him an early-morning bath. She'd been desperate for something to do, anything to take her away from her terrified thoughts.

She was going to marry Alessio Palvetti.

When it came down to it, what choice did she have? Either she married him or she lost Dom for good.

Restless, she swiped through her phone's photo album until she found one of Domenico and Caroline. It had been taken at a music festival the weekend after they'd married when Caroline had been three months pregnant.

They'd been so excited about the pregnancy, blissfully unaware that only two months later their happiness would be torn apart by Caroline's diagnosis. That diagnosis had been the spur that had forced them into writing their wills and nominating Beth as their unborn child's guardian.

Caroline had had no blood family left. Domenico had plenty of relatives but he'd hated the lot of them. He'd hated everything about his childhood and the straitjacket it had put him in and vowed his own children would never suffer as he had. His children would be raised to value decency and kindness and encouraged to follow their dreams. They would not worship at the altar of the almighty money tree. They would not be raised by strangers and starved of affection by their parents. They would not be indoctrinated into believing that the family's business and reputation was worth more than them. They would never be thrown out and cut off for the crime of being different.

In Domenico's eyes, Alessio had been worse than the rest of the Palvettis put together. And Beth would have to marry him.

For all that Beth adored her job, the world she'd entered as an eighteen-year-old virgin had left her as jaded about love and relationships as it had made her distrustful of rich men. As far as she could see, relationships didn't exist, only sexual conquests. She'd been so envious of the love Caroline and Domenico had found with each other but witnessing it first-hand had also given her hope. If they could find that kind of love in this disposable world then she could find it with someone too. Mr Right was out there somewhere, a kind, decent man she could trust and give her heart to and create a future with.

She would never meet Mr Right now. Her future was tied to a monster, a man who encompassed everything she'd spent her adult life avoiding. Her future would be spent trapped in a loveless marriage with a man who saw her as a business associate and future carrier for his heirs.

Her brain burned to imagine sharing a bed with him to create those heirs, and burned even harder to remember how amazing it had felt to be spun in his arms when she had believed him to be someone else. And that dream she'd had…

She hated him for that. His pretence had opened her up to an attraction she had never felt before, a desire that would never have sprung to life had she known who he really was.

She stared at the picture again and rubbed

her finger lightly over Caroline's happy face. 'I'm sorry. I underestimated him.'

Maybe this really was for the best, she told herself, valiantly trying to find the positives. Dom would grow up with unimaginable wealth and have all the advantages that came with it, all the things that Beth couldn't give to him as a single parent. Marriage to Alessio meant Dom would still have her there by his side, loving him and instilling the values his parents had wanted him to grow up with.

Caroline had made the ultimate sacrifice to protect Dom and enable him to have a long, healthy life. She'd given *her* life. Compared to that, Beth sacrificing her future to ensure that protection continued was nothing.

CHAPTER FIVE

ALESSIO'S HOME TURNED out to be a seventeenth-century baroque villa set in a huge estate complete with its own lake on the outskirts of Milan.

Beth tried hard not to look impressed when the huge iron gates opened and the villa was revealed in all its glory but she was unable to stop her jaw dropping in stunned awe. It was L-shaped and three storeys high, topped with a terracotta roof. The ground floor was ringed by a magnificent colonnade of intricately carved stone pillars.

This was going to be her home?

'How long have you lived here?' she asked when she'd got out of the car and had removed Dom's car seat. After having screamed the entire journey on Alessio's private jet—watching Alessio shove plugs into his ears and his face grimace as he'd tried to work over the racket had given Beth a perverse sense of enjoyment—the baby had fallen asleep the moment their car had set into motion. She didn't want to risk waking him.

'All my life. My parents transferred it into my name four years ago when they retired and I took over the running of Palvetti.'

'Where do they live now?'

'When he's not travelling the world, my father lives in a villa by Lake Como. My mother died six months ago.'

She blinked. 'I'm sorry. I didn't know that.'

He took his briefcase from his driver with a nod of thanks. 'Her death is the reason I tried to find my brother. I thought he deserved to know. If only someone had shown us the same courtesy when Domenico died, I wouldn't have had to find out through a private investigator.'

He then lifted Dom's car seat with the sleeping baby still in it and strode to the front door, his subtle rebuke slicing through her chest.

She remembered asking Caroline if she was going to notify Domenico's Italian family about his death and the violent shake of her head as she'd refused. She'd been terrified that they'd try and take his body from her and have him buried in Milan. With all the heartbreak and devastation they'd been coping with, Beth had soon forgotten all about the Palvetti family's ignorance of their son's and brother's death.

She wished she hadn't forgotten. Monster or not, no one should have to learn about the death of a family member the way Alessio had, and at a time when he must already have been reeling from his mother's death.

'I really am sorry,' she called, hurrying to his side before he could open the door.

She prevented her hand from instinctively touching his arm in comfort by the skin of her teeth.

Hard emerald eyes met hers.

'About your mother,' she clarified. 'I know what it's like to lose a parent. It's hard.'

'You have lost a parent?' The softening of the emeralds as he asked this made her realise he'd spoken the truth about having had his investigators only dig into the past five years of her life.

'Mine died a long time ago.'

His brow furrowed slightly. 'Both of them?'

She nodded.

He held her gaze for the longest time. 'I'm sorry.'

But then the door they were standing at was opened for them and the brief softening between them gone.

All Beth's morbid thoughts were swept away the moment she stepped into the reception room.

The interior of Alessio's home was even more impressive than the exterior and Beth was taken back to the time she had first stepped into the Viennese palace and had imagined herself a princess.

Had it really been only a day ago she'd had that feeling?

If the palace was the place where a princess had experienced her first ball, this was the place the princess would call home.

Her awe slowly transformed into terror as the richness of her surroundings became even clearer.

History seeped through the frescoed walls of the rooms Alessio led her through and, with the uniformed staff lined up to greet her arrival, she had the surreal feeling that she'd slipped back to a time when men duelled for a woman's honour.

A fish out of water would have felt more at home here than she ever could.

What would it be like to grow up in such a place?

Beth's early childhood home with her parents had been a small terraced house. After their death when she was nine she'd lived with her foster parents in a house only marginally bigger. It was in that home she had met Caroline.

What fun they would have had in this villa that should really be called a castle. She imagined them as they'd been then, zooming around on roller-skates, trashing the buffed stone flooring, careering into the original sculptures, paintings and highly polished furniture lining the rooms.

From what Domenico had told her, she doubted either he or Alessio had been allowed such freedom. Her childhood might have had its heartbreak but at least she'd had a childhood. Palvetti children spent theirs being indoctrinated into the family business.

Once all the staff introductions had been done with, she followed Alessio up the wide stairs to the first floor.

'This will be your room until our wedding,' he informed her as he opened a door.

If her heart hadn't made such a thud at what he'd left unsaid, that come their wedding night she would share a room with him, she would have gasped at the first sight of the room.

The bed was huge and covered in a beautifully embroidered golden bedspread. All the furniture, from the bedside tables to the dressing table to the *chaise longue* spread beneath the huge window, was carved from a gorgeous deep reddish wood she'd never seen before. The walls were skimmed a cream colour but the ceiling was frescoed with ancient cherubs.

'Domenico's room adjoins it.' He briskly opened a connecting door to reveal a room with the same proportions as hers but furnished and decorated for an infant. He placed the sleeping baby's car seat on the floor by the cot.

'Did you get this done for him?' she asked, suddenly desperate to talk about anything so as not to think that at some point in her near future she would have to share a bed with Alessio.

He'd made it very clear that he wanted a real

marriage and equally clear that that entailed sharing a bed.

It was a thought that sent awareness firing through her, making her veins heat like molasses.

'It's always been a nursery. That door...' he pointed '...adjoins the nanny's room. Miranda will arrive in the morning.'

'She was your spy?'

'No, but I have offered her a permanent position.'

'When do you expect me to start work for you?' If Miranda was coming here tomorrow he must want her to start soon.

The thought made her head swim.

A lot of things were making her head spin. Everything had happened so quickly the night before that it was only as the day went on that the ramifications of what she'd agreed to had really hit home.

Palvetti was one of the most iconic and exclusive brands in the world. The family behind it was one of the richest and most elusive. How could Alessio expect her to fit into the business or with his family? She knew nothing about jewellery or fragrances. She didn't speak their language. She didn't believe in packing small children away to boarding school.

Yes, a fish out of water would fit in better.

'I will introduce you to the business after our wedding.' He made it sound like a living, breathing entity.

'And when will that be?'

'On Wednesday. Everything is arranged. I think it is best if Domenico remain with Miranda during the service.'

She nodded her agreement and stared down at her ward, oblivious in his slumber to the huge changes happening to his world. She would be his only constant.

She rubbed her arms and decided it was good they were marrying so quickly. The sooner, the better. Get the wedding over with before Alessio realised what a terrible fit for him she was, changed his mind and sent her packing.

'Can you please stop calling him "Domenico"?' she asked. This was one thing she couldn't wait until their wedding day to resolve. Every time he called him that, it grated. 'His name is Dom.'

'His birth certificate has him named as Domenico.'

'That was your brother's name. Caroline named him that to honour him but she wanted him to be known as Dom.'

Alessio stared hard into the chocolate eyes that, on the dance floor of the palace only the evening before, had been as soft as warmed caramel.

He had never met his sister-in-law. She had thought so badly of the Palvettis that not only had she failed to tell them of her husband's death but she'd failed to give her son their family name, choosing instead to give him her maiden name.

If his brother had been alive he would have pinned him against a wall and shaken him until his teeth rattled for all the heinous lies he must have told about them.

But his brother was dead and his sister-in-law had met her death only six months later. She was not here to fight for her right to insist her son be called the name she wished.

Going against his every inclination, Alessio jerked a nod. 'I will try to remember.'

Beth's shoulders lowered. 'Thank you.'

'I will have the chef prepare some lunch for us and then my lawyer is coming here so we can get the pre-nuptial agreement signed.' He placed his briefcase on her dresser and opened it. 'Here's the draft copy for you to read. Would you like me to give you the basic points of it?'

She stared at the document in his hands with suspicion then gave a sharp nod.

He paused a moment before speaking again. The situation at the palace had been far more emotional than Alessio had anticipated and he'd been aware Beth had agreed to their marriage under duress. This was the moment, when emotions were calmer, when the final cards would be laid on the table and the deal between them would be either sewn up or broken irrevocably.

'The contract states in black and white that in the event of a divorce I get full custody rights over Domenico... Dom. It also prevents you from speaking about any aspect of our marriage or the business.'

A flash of angry colour stained her cheeks. 'That's hardly fair.'

'Only if you divorce me.'

The colour deepened and her brow furrowed. 'If I sign it, then you can divorce me and get automatic custody of Dom without any protracted legal battle?'

'I would already have custody of him if that was all I wanted.'

She made a sound like a laugh but the expression on her face showed she was far from amused. 'This is all about keeping your name out of the press.' She took a step back and hugged her arms across her chest. 'If I sign this contract then I am effectively gagged—you can divorce me on a whim and banish me from Dom's life and there would be nothing I could do about it.'

'Palvettis do not divorce.'

'Forgive me if I'm unable to take anything you say at face value.'

'There has been only one divorce in my family since the business was formed.' He fought the anger building inside him. He knew that gaining her trust was something he would have to work on but her attitude still bit. 'That divorce came this close...' he put a thumb and forefinger together '...to destroying everything. Not one Palvetti has married since without a cast-iron pre-nuptial agreement. We protect ourselves. I don't believe in divorce but this contract protects me and my nephew if you choose to divorce me, and it protects you too—

it provides you with ten million euros for every year of our marriage.'

'That's not protection!' she cried, throwing her hands in the air. 'I don't care about the money, I care about Dom. He belongs with me and you know it.'

Alessio gritted his teeth and ran a hand through his hair. 'Dom belongs here in Milan. The business could one day be his. We're his family.'

'*I'm* his family.'

He looked her in the eye. 'You're not blood.'

'How dare you?' Her face drained of colour but then she straightened and paced towards him, the anger coming off her almost a visual wave. 'Caroline and I were foster sisters from when we were both still in primary school. We thought of ourselves as real sisters and I loved her. Dom's lived with me since his birth—I was there *at* his birth. I changed his first nappy. I gave him his first bottle. I held Caroline in my arms when she took her last breath and I promised her that I would always protect him.'

Now she stood before him, rising on her toes to eyeball him. 'I might not share the same blood as Dom, but I love him more than life itself, so don't you ever say I disqualify from being his family just because I don't share his blood.'

He stared into the furious, beautiful face and felt the strangest compression in his chest.

When he'd first discovered a young woman had guardianship of his nephew he'd assumed Domenico had chosen her out of spite for his family. It was unthinkable to give custody of a child to a stranger when there was blood family willing and able to take him.

His investigators had shown Beth and Caroline had shared a flat before Caroline's marriage to Domenico, and that Caroline had moved back into that flat after his death, but he'd had no idea their history went back such a long way or that they'd been foster sisters.

No wonder Beth had such deep, protective feelings for his nephew.

Instinct had him place a hand to her cheek. It was the first time he'd touched her since their dance.

Her eyes widened and she seemed to freeze.

'*Bella*, I understand you love Dom, but it doesn't change that he's a Palvetti by blood and he belongs here. If you want what's best for him then you must see that.' He rubbed a thumb down the length of her cheekbone. Even the finest silk could not feel so good.

She shivered. The movement was so slight he would have missed it had he not been paying such close attention.

He brought his face closer to hers, catching her scent, welcoming its dive into his senses and its settling into his bloodstream.

Marriage to a woman who didn't elicit his desire was unthinkable and Beth elicited it in a way he had never experienced before. There was a charge between them that buzzed through his skin to his veins.

He felt another quiver escape her but her eyes remained unblinking on his.

'I don't know what poison my brother filled your head with about me and nor do I want to know. I have enough bad feelings towards him without adding to it and any defence I give will be nothing but meaningless words. But I promise you this. I will be a good husband to you.'

Her voice when she finally spoke hardly rose above a whisper. 'But you get all the power.'

'I am not marrying you on a whim.' He moved his hand round the back of her hair and splayed his fingers through the silky strands, watching the colour stain her cheeks. 'I have gone to great lengths to ensure your suitability but even if I am proved wrong I will never divorce you.'

Her eyes continued to bore into him, unblinking, but her voice gained in strength. 'Then prove it by giving me custody of Dom if you do. Make it fair. You're taking everything else—give me that one small comfort for my own peace of mind.'

He stared back hard. Trust and respect needed to be built between them and what she asked was not unreasonable.

He inhaled through his nostrils, filling his greedy lungs with more of her scent, and nodded. *'Va bene.'*

'What does that mean?'

'It means okay. I will get my lawyer to change that clause.'

Her chest rose. 'If you divorce me I get custody of Dom?'

'*Si*. Yes. But if you divorce me, I get custody of him.'

Finally, the chocolate eyes blinked. He only realised how tightly she'd been holding herself when her shoulders loosened almost imperceptibly.

As if he knew his future had been decided in that moment, Dom stirred and made a sound like a smothered wail.

The sound cut through the atmosphere between them like a bursting balloon.

Beth blinked again and stepped back, out of his reach, her gaze now on the floor. Fresh colour crawled over her face and she tucked a lock of hair behind her ear.

Dom gave another wail.

Alessio, anticipating the screams that were sure to follow the child's awakening, made himself scarce.

Later, when they were with his lawyer and going through the finer details of the contract, Alessio spotted something on his shirt. He plucked it with his fingers. It was a long, dark hair.

He looked from the hair to the woman it belonged to, her head bowed with concentration, and thrilled to know that in three short days that glorious hair would be spilled over his pillow.

Her eyes suddenly looked up from the contract and met his gaze and he felt that charge pulse between them again.

Colour suffused her cheeks and she hastily dropped her gaze back to the document.

He smothered a smile.

It wouldn't be only his pillow that hair spilled over. It would be him too.

CHAPTER SIX

MIRANDA ARRIVED EARLY the next morning. Beth's relief at her arrival was heartfelt. She hardly knew the nanny but her presence in the sprawling villa soothed her, made her think, probably wrongly, that she had an ally in this new life of hers.

Her first night under Alessio's roof had been awful. It had taken hours to fall asleep, her mind a whirl of thoughts and fears. When she'd awoken to Dom's babbling from his cot, she'd fortified herself with the strength she'd found when she'd signed that damnable contract.

She was here. This was going to be her life. Moping around or letting anger fester would not solve or change anything. If she was making this commitment then she owed it to Dom and herself to make the best of it.

Beth was good at starting over. She'd done it when her parents had died and she'd had to move fifty miles away from everything she'd ever known. That distance had felt huge.

She'd started over again too when she'd moved to London with Caroline: eighteen years old and armed with nothing but a small bag of clothing and enough money saved from her Saturday job to rent a room in a hostel. She'd made the best of it and within a year had earned enough to put down a deposit on the flat that she would now have to give up.

She thought of that small bag of clothing when Alessio handed her a credit card before he left for work and told her to buy herself a new wardrobe of clothes and whatever else she needed.

As she was already out of clean clothes, this was one order she was not going to argue with. With the nanny in situ taking care of Dom, a member of Alessio's household staff drove her to Via Montenapoleone.

After a year of frugality—buying clothes only when absolutely necessary and even then making her purchases in charity shops—to suddenly find herself in a street packed with designer stores and boutiques was overwhelming.

She spent more on clothes in her first two

hours there than she had spent in her entire life but there was little enjoyment. She hadn't known when she'd packed the faded jeans and simple top, spare clothing in case Dom was sick on her, that she would wear them on the first major shopping expedition of her life or that she would feel so shabby in them.

There was no escaping the presence of the man who had tricked his way into her life and brought her here either.

After a quick break for lunch, she wandered around the beauty department of one the most exclusive designer shops and stumbled on a Palvetti concession staffed by an ethereal beauty. There were no price tags on any of the scents displayed in packaging so beautiful she guessed it must cost as much as the scents themselves to produce.

Curiosity made her spray her wrists with one of the perfumes. She sniffed and sighed with pleasure at the wonderful aroma filling her senses. If it had been any other brand she would have added it to her purchases with the crème bath and shower gel of the same scent.

After that, she found she kept sniffing her wrist.

Later, she found a Palvetti jewellery store tucked away discreetly in a side street and found herself blown away by the beauty and craftsmanship of the items. No wonder their jewellery was so coveted. As with their perfumes, there were no price tags, and she felt too self-conscious at her shabbiness to ask.

Leaving the jewellers, she went off to buy a load of mercifully guilt-free clothes and toys for Dom.

Then it was time to make her final purchase. An outfit to marry in.

She chose the first suitable dress she came across and tried not to think too hard that in only two days she would wear it and exchange her vows with Alessio.

In two nights, she would share his bed.

She squeezed her eyes shut and tried, again, to push the thought from her mind. If she let it settle...

In defiance of herself, in defiance of the man forcing this life on her, she bought another pair of shoes.

Laden with designer bags, she returned to the villa and went straight to the nursery. Miranda helped her put all of Dom's new purchases away then went off for her dinner while Beth gave him a bath. Bath time had always been a favourite part of Dom's routine, ending with snuggles on the sofa, a bottle of his formula milk and a book.

She'd just taken him out of the bath and wrapped him in a towel on the change mat when she heard a noise in the nursery. From her vantage point on the bathroom floor, she called out, 'Miranda, do you know where Dom's tractor book is? It was in his change bag but I don't remember seeing it earlier.'

Beth's heart slammed when the figure that appeared in the bathroom doorway was the looming figure of Alessio rather than the kindly nanny.

'I don't know anything about a tractor book but Miranda will be up in a few minutes. She's making Dom's milk,' he said drolly.

She stared up at him for a moment, hot blood whooshing in her head, then hurriedly reached for a nappy. Hell's bells, her hands were *shaking*.

She'd thought she had a few more hours free of him.

'How has your day been?' he asked.

'Expensive.' It was all she could get out of her tightened throat. One glimpse of him and her equilibrium went to pieces.

Alessio watched his nephew grab hold of his foot and try and shove it in his mouth.

Beth's handling of him was masterful. She put the nappy on the fidgety child and fastened it expertly in seconds.

'Did you get everything you need?' he asked.

She nodded and grabbed something he recognised as an all-in-one baby's sleep-suit neatly laid on the bathroom chair beside her.

Alessio found it fascinating to watch her manipulate Dom into it. He'd never seen a baby be dressed before. It was far more complicated than he would have supposed, mostly on account of Dom's wriggling limbs, but her pretty hands managed it deftly.

'What did you want the book for?'

'To read to him.' Her fingers now worked on the poppers of the sleep-suit.

'He likes being read to?' he asked dubiously.

'It's part of his bedtime routine.'

'Can he understand the words?'

'I doubt it.'

'Then why bother?'

'Because it's soothing for him. Children are never too young to discover their love of words.' With Dom now dressed, she got to her feet and scooped him up. 'Can you take him while I look for the book, please?'

'Me?' He'd never held a child in his life. That was what nannies and other childcare workers were for.

She gave him a look that showed how unimpressed she was and thrust his nephew forward to him.

'How do I hold him?'

'Upright is usually the best way.' Was that amusement he heard in her voice? 'His neck doesn't need supporting any more so, as long as you don't drop him, you won't break him… *Don't* drop him.'

Alessio took the child from her, holding him around the waist and raising him up to look at his beaming face as he carried him from the bathroom into the nursery.

The little legs kicked out as if Dom were riding an imaginary bike, the chubby face tilting from side to side.

When he sat down on the armchair, his

nephew placed his feet on Alessio's lap and immediately started bouncing.

He laughed. Dom laughed too, his bright-blue eyes shining.

Domenico had had blue eyes.

Domenico would never hold his son on his lap...

The thought made his heart clench so tightly he almost doubled over with the pain from it.

He looked at Beth, on her hands and knees going through the dresser drawers, and his heart clenched even tighter.

Alessio's mother had been a wonderful woman but, like all Palvetti women, not in the slightest bit maternal. It was the way things had to be, he'd always accepted that, and it had never bothered him the way it had his brother. The mundane task of raising children had been taken by nannies, the parents there to guide them into being hard working, conscientious young people able to step up and take their place in the family business.

Beth had the hard working and conscientious traits mastered but she also had a huge maternal streak running through her. Where had that come from? Raising Dom? Or an influence from her own upbringing?

He remembered the glimmer of pain he'd seen in her eyes when she'd told him she'd lost her own parents. He knew nothing about their deaths.

There was so much to discover about the woman he was marrying.

She pulled a small square book out of the bottom drawer. 'Found it!'

She scrambled to her feet and walked over to lift Dom from Alessio's lap. As she did so, a lock of her loose hair brushed against his cheek.

A hand he had no control of reached out and gripped her waist.

She sucked in a breath that stilled on her lips. Frozen for long moments, her gaze slowly dropped down to meet his.

Ages passed where all they did was stare into each other's eyes.

He took in the cheeks heightened with colour, the parted lips…

Awareness shot through him. Awareness for this delectable creature that in two short days would be his.

He forced a deep breath into his lungs and, keeping his hand on her waist, rose to his feet.

Stepping so close that the tip of her breast brushed against his chest, he breathed in the scent of her hair and was assailed with thoughts of marshmallows.

The tiniest quiver escaped from her.

He stepped back and placed his thumb on lips as plump and delicious as the marshmallows her hair smelt of.

Her wide eyes stayed locked on his.

Were it not for the child in her arms it would be his mouth on those lips. And she would be in his arms.

He dropped his thumb from the mouth he ached to devour and stepped away from temptation.

'I will see you at dinner, *bella*,' he murmured.

She blinked rapidly then gave the briefest of nods in acknowledgement.

As Alessio strode down the corridor to his room, willing the ache in his loins to ease just a little so as to become bearable, he thought their wedding night couldn't come soon enough.

The anticipation might just kill him.

* * *

Beth inhaled the new scents that filled the night air as she walked the path towards Alessio's lake. Water shimmered beneath the moonlight as far as the eye could see, and a small white cottage stood to the left of the lake at the top of the path which she hadn't noticed before. Not that there had been much time for exploring. The two nights and three days she'd already spent under Alessio's roof had slipped away as if time had been turbo-charged.

Since he'd walked in on Dom's bedtime routine, she'd seen little of him.

His absence had been in body only.

He was never far from her mind.

She couldn't stop thinking about him. Everything she did, everywhere she went, his face haunted her like a spectre.

The times when she was with him were worse.

She'd become aware of his every movement. When they'd shared their evening meals she'd been aware of his every sip of wine, every slice of his knife, the movement of his throat when he'd swallowed his food...

Tonight it had got so bad that she'd refused

any dessert, made the excuse that she was tired and retired to her bedroom early.

It would be the last time she slept alone.

She should feel nothing but dread.

The anticipation she had felt before the ball, which even with all that had been going on she had known was for Alessio—or Valente, as she'd believed him to be—was nothing like the anticipation that now coiled through every cell in her body.

Was it any wonder she'd been unable to sleep?

This was worse than her first night here before she'd woken with the resolve to make the best of everything.

After hours spent staring at the cherubs on the ceiling above her head, listening to the noises of the villa gradually reduce to silence as everyone went to bed, her own head refusing to join the silence, she'd realised sleep was impossible. Every fear had crawled out from where she'd buried it to plague her.

She'd needed to clear her head.

Now she spotted a wooden bridge that spanned the width of a relatively narrow section of the lake. She walked to the middle of it and peered over the railing into the blackness.

'I hope you're not planning to jump. It's twenty feet deep there.'

Alessio's voice, which cut through the stillness of the air, made her jump.

She watched his silhouette approach and put a hand to her suddenly thundering heart. She'd never seen him in jeans before. The pair he wore fit snugly and the dark T-shirt they were topped with emphasised the muscularity of his physique.

Even in the dark he was strikingly gorgeous.

She inhaled and turned her gaze away from him. 'Are you following me?'

'I heard you leave and was curious where you were going.'

'I couldn't sleep.'

Beth guessed that him being awake at this time meant he couldn't sleep either.

'Nervous?' he asked lightly.

'Terrified. Aren't you?' She wasn't making this commitment alone.

'No.' He joined her at the centre of the bridge and put his hands on the railings beside hers.

She caught a fresh citrusy scent that had her stomach flipping over in a loop and made her think of long, hot showers.

She tightened her hold and breathed through her mouth.

For a long time, neither of them spoke.

'Doesn't it bother you at *all* that you're committing your life to a loveless marriage?' she asked.

'Palvettis don't marry for love.'

The nonchalance of his answer bugged her as much as the actual words. 'Never?'

'The only Palvetti who has married for love since the Second World War is my uncle Giuseppe and he is the only Palvetti to have divorced. That is no coincidence.'

'What happened?'

'His wife couldn't handle coming second to the business. After three years of marriage, she had enough and left him. Things got nasty.'

'In what way?'

'At the time Palvetti were in the process of buying into an Australian mining company. They'd discovered an area with an abundance of corundum—that's the mineral from which you get sapphires and rubies. No one else knew of the site. My uncle was the chief negotiator in the deal so Giulia, his wife, was aware of all the details. She blackmailed us. The equivalent of fifty million euros in today's money for her silence or she would sell her knowledge to one of our rivals.'

'Did you pay it?'

'We did, and we hit her with a water-tight contract that would have seen her ruined if she broke the terms. She didn't care. All she wanted was the money and to humiliate the family she had come to detest. I was a child when it happened but we all learned our lesson from it. It's why we go to such great lengths to protect ourselves and the business. Everything is intricately linked: the family, the business and our fortune. Marrying for love is dangerous. Emotions are messy and best kept separate.'

She soaked this new information in. 'Okay, so it makes sense to protect yourselves after that, but what about the spouses? Do they know what they're signing up for when they marry one of you?'

'Always. We select spouses who are familiar with us and who we know well and who we know will fit in and play their part. People with the same mindset as us.'

'How do your family feel about me becoming a part of it? They don't know me.'

He took a moment before answering. 'They trust my judgement.'

It was an evasive answer but she didn't push it. She would learn for herself what the rest of his family felt about her joining them.

'I don't have their mindset,' she warned him quietly. 'I'm not like any of you. Until I took guardianship of Dom, I was career-minded, but it wasn't the be-all and end-all for me like your business is with you... Don't you feel *any* guilt that you're locking me into a loveless marriage?'

She felt his eyes fix on her but kept her own gaze on the black expanse of water surrounding them.

'Marrying you is a gamble.' His tone was meditative. 'There were three other women I'd had my eye on as a potential future wife. Any one of them would have accepted my proposal and they would have fitted into Palvetti seamlessly. I could have taken Dom from you and raised him with one of those women but I didn't. What I *did* do was take a huge amount of my time away from the business to give you a chance and see if you were suitable. You have no lover that you're leaving behind. You are coming into this marriage with nothing and I am prepared to give you everything—a beautiful home, great wealth, a fulfilling career and a continued role and influence in Dom's life.'

Three other women?

Beth had thought there was nothing Alessio could do or say that would shock her but that revelation...

How would he have chosen one? Played Ip Dip Do?

She couldn't bring herself to ask. Nausea churned deep in her stomach but her head felt light.

Somehow Alessio had managed to make any question of guilt seem like an affront, make it seem that he was doing her a favour...

It dawned on her that he genuinely believed he was.

And maybe he was right to.

Until that point Beth had only thought about their marriage in terms of everything she was having to give up: her job and her home. Alessio truly was taking the gamble he'd stated by marrying her.

He was giving up a future with a wife who

was a certainty so that she and Dom could always be together.

She rolled her neck to ease the tension in it then shifted her body to face him. 'Those women you spoke of…were you…lovers with any of them?'

It was the first time she'd ever uttered the word 'lover'. Until Alessio had casually mentioned a moment ago that she had no lover to leave behind, she'd never heard it from another's lips, had thought it a word only used in books.

He shook his head.

'Do you have a current lover I should know about?' She was proud of herself for the nonchalance of her tone as she bandied the word around a second time.

If one word encapsulated the Palvetti brand, it was sophistication. If she was going to fit into his world, as she knew she must, she would have to learn it, and that meant learning a language that was so much more than linguistic translation. There was something sophisticated about the term 'lover', a wholly different connotation to 'boyfriend', 'girlfriend' or 'partner'.

The glimmer of a smile played on his lips.

He lifted a hand to rub his thumb against her chin. 'No. There is only one woman who has captured my attention in recent months and I am marrying her tomorrow.'

The gleam that shone from his eyes and the sensation careering over her skin at his touch killed stone-dead the next question she was about to ask.

She tried her hardest to breathe but her heart had expanded so greatly it crushed her lungs into nothing.

How could it be like this? Every time Alessio touched her she melted for him. Every time he entered a room her heart crashed into her ribs.

Her feelings for him went against all logic. The truth of his identity should have killed her fledging desire but the opposite had happened. The more time she spent with him, the greater her awareness of all the new feelings being evoked within her. And the greater her awareness of the danger these feelings posed.

Theirs could never be a real marriage as she knew marriages to be. Her parents had been young and often stupid but their marriage had been real. She remembered ferocious arguments and tears, but she also remembered them holding hands whenever they went out, remembered their affectionate kisses, the sneaky bottom-squeezes and the laughter... She remembered the love. Her foster parents had been far more restrained with their affection but she remembered reading the cards they had exchanged on birthdays and Valentine's and the messages of love written in them.

And she remembered another couple who had loved each other wholeheartedly.

She took a deep breath and moved back. 'You know what I don't understand?'

'What?'

'How you can say all this stuff about the business and family being so important and intricately linked when you kicked your own brother out of it. Was it because he refused to comply with the business-comes-first line?'

CHAPTER SEVEN

WHITE NOISE FILLED Alessio's ears at this unexpected turn of the conversation.

'He said that?' he asked slowly. 'Domenico
said we kicked him out?'

'He said that *you* did. He said that, when your
parents retired and you became the boss of Palvetti, the first thing you did was kick him out
of the home and cut his income off.'

A swell of anger rose inside him. It had taken
no effort at all to imagine his brother spreading
poison about him but hearing outright lies…

'Tell me everything,' he said grimly. 'Everything he said about me and my family.'

He'd never wanted to waste his breath de-
fending himself but could see that letting this
go would mean his brother's allegations always
hanging over them.

'Okay…' He heard Beth take a sharp breath
before the words spilled out. 'In a nutshell, he
said his entire life was spent being groomed to

be someone he never wanted to be. His dream of being a musician was opposed and hindered because you didn't want the Palvetti name associated with anything other than its core brands. He said living in the Palvetti household was like being straitjacketed from birth, and that all any of you ever cared about was the business, and that money, possessions and the family name were more important than your own blood's mental health. He never felt loved or wanted for himself.'

As soon as Beth had blurted it all out she turned her head to look at him.

She could read nothing from Alessio's expression. It was as if a mask of his face had been placed over the real one. The only life on the mask was the pulse throbbing in his temple.

Eventually he rolled his neck and grimaced. 'I cannot comment on Domenico's feelings but the rest of it is a lie.' He pointed at the white cottage by the side of the lake. 'Have you been in there yet?'

She shook her head.

'Domenico moved into it when he left school. Our parents paid to have a music studio installed in it for him. The studio's still there.

They were disappointed that he didn't want to join the business but supported his decision. Their only stipulation was that he use a pseudonym if he made it big, but he never made any money off his music.'

His laughter echoed bitterly in the stillness of the night. 'When I took the helm of Palvetti he was twenty-eight years old, and still chasing the dream, and still turning his nose up at the family business that had supported his lazy lifestyle for all those years. I offered him a job working in the creative department. He could have done any number of things. He could have worked on the advertising campaigns, because I do not deny my brother had a brilliant mind, but he wanted none of it.'

Beth listened hard to this emotionless retelling of a story that flipped on its head Domenico's perspective.

'Our parents signed the villa and the land it stood on to me. Domenico was angry that this included his cottage—he thought it should have been given to him. I gave him some home truths.' His mouth twisted. 'If he wanted the cottage, then he had to earn it. Either join the business or find the funds to pay for it some other way because he had leeched off the rest of us for long enough. We argued… In truth it was the most ferocious argument we'd ever had. Our parents tried to calm things and Domenico turned on them. He called our mother a name not to be repeated in polite society and that was when I told him to get out because I was this close…' he put his thumb and first finger together, 'to hitting him. He left that night. I expected him to come back the next day but he didn't. He changed his phone and closed his social media accounts. He cut us off so effectively that he'd been dead for a year before I knew of it.'

His lips tightened and he shook his head before emitting another bitter, disbelieving laugh. 'I did not throw him out of his home—he left. And, as for cutting his income off, what was I supposed to do? He rejected us and everything we stood for. Why give him more money when he'd left with no forwarding address and when he considered us bourgeois bastards? He was given all the freedom and creativity he wanted and a healthy allowance he did nothing to earn. It was not our fault he didn't have the talent to go with the ideals.'

He turned back to face her. When he met her gaze, his expression softened a touch. Reaching out to capture a lock of her hair, he said, 'I don't expect you to take me at my word—it's too soon for that—but I do ask you give me the benefit of the doubt. Can you do that?'

She held his gaze, wishing she could see the expression in his eyes better, but the darkness of the night shadowed it.

Alessio's version of events countered everything Domenico had said but he'd spoken with such conviction that she found herself believing him, which in turn made her feel like a complete traitor.

'I'll try,' she whispered then, because she had to say it, 'But I need you to promise me that you won't let your loathing of Domenico affect how you treat his son.'

He released his hold on her hair and dragged his fingers through his curls with a groan. 'Beth, I am not a monster. Dom is innocent of everything. One promise I can make is that I will treat him as I would if he were my own son and that I will do everything in my power to make you both feel a part of this family.'

Then he turned and walked away.

Beth watched his silhouette vanish into the dark as he crossed the bridge, utterly torn.

Later, when she was back in bed for what would be the last time alone, the thought that crowded her mind before sleep finally came for her was that, truth or lie, monster or not, none of that mattered. It didn't change anything. She would marry him regardless and, whatever direction their marriage took, however well she embraced the role she'd been given, the one thing she would never have was the love she had always hoped one day to find.

The driver stopped the car by Piazza del Duomo, the vast square right in the beating heart of Milan, and opened the door for them.

Tourists were out in force that sunny afternoon, cameras and phones flashing shots of the Duomo, Milan's famous cathedral, and the impressive statue of Vittorio Emmanuel II, the first King of a united Italy.

Before getting out of the car, Alessio gazed over at the statue, the King on his horse aloft on its marble pedestal and mighty plinth, and thought Vittorio had had an easier time uniting Italy than he would have uniting his family behind the idea of Beth Hardingstone as a Palvetti.

Her question as to what his family thought about her had been astute but he'd kept his answer evasive. She had enough to contend with without him feeding her fears.

Usually Palvetti marriages were a cause of great celebration but bringing a stranger into the fold had caused mutterings of discontent. Beth was an unknown quantity to the rest of the family. She'd been too good a friend of Domenico, who had hated them all so much, to be trusted. If they knew the poisonous lies Domenico had fed her, they would distrust her even more.

He had no intention of sharing that with them.

Beth now had the facts of Domenico's life as a Palvetti rather than his brother's twisted, self-serving version of events. He had to trust she would be as good as her word and give him the benefit of the doubt, and his family too.

And he had to trust that his family would keep their word and give Beth the benefit of doubt in turn.

He turned his gaze from Vittorio's statue

and looked again at the woman he was minutes from tying himself to.

She'd chosen a figure-hugging cream lace dress that managed to be bridal yet sophisticated, falling to just below her knees. She'd plaited her dark hair into a coiled bun at the nape of her neck.

His breath had caught in his throat when she'd descended the villa's stairs towards him and it caught again now.

Her beauty grew every time he looked at her.

Beth followed him out of the car and stared at the Duomo. 'Are we marrying *there*?'

'No. That would attract too much attention to us. We're marrying in the royal palace.' He pointed to the right of the Duomo, at the Palazzo Reale.

She swallowed.

'It's not a real palace,' he told her with a grin. 'It's the palace Milan used to be governed from and now it's a place of culture. It also hosts civil wedding ceremonies.'

She was silent as they took the short walk to the palace, silent as they were taken to the second floor and silent as they entered the Sala degli Specchi hall.

Alessio had chosen this location specifically. He needed a quick wedding to tie Beth to him, so that had put paid to a large traditional wedding, but he still wanted the ceremony to have some meaning and be an event to remember.

They were pledging their lives together. Whatever the circumstances that had brought them together, their vows would be real and he wanted them to feel real to her too.

This beautiful room, with its seventeenth-century tapestry, gold-framed mirrors and brocade-covered chairs, had a far greater elegance and richness than an ordinary civil wedding venue. It gave their wedding the gravitas it needed.

He felt Beth stiffen at his side as she took in the number of people who'd already filed into the room. Every single one was a Palvetti. Beth didn't have one person from her side to wish her well.

Her parents were dead but what about the rest of her family? He'd asked during dinner on her first night here if she wanted to invite anyone but she'd shaken her head and then excused herself to check on Dom.

Only now, seeing the lop-sidedness of the guest list, did he wish he'd asked her again.

He reached for her hand and squeezed it. 'Don't worry,' he whispered in an undertone. 'They don't bite.'

He felt the slightest squeeze back.

Through the crowd of Palvettis craning their necks to get a good look at the bride, to his delight he spotted his father and uncle in the front row. It had been touch and go if they would make it back from the Caribbean in time for the ceremony.

His father caught his eye and winked at him,

But there was no time for introductions. Not yet.

Beth found herself struggling to breathe.

She hadn't imagined so many people would be there. And they were all Palvettis. She hadn't realised just how large his family was.

She had no one.

She felt as alone as she had in that first awful year after her parents had died, before Caroline had come into her life and brought some sunshine into it.

As the years had passed, the pain of their loss had lessened by degrees, but today she felt their absence like a physical ache and wished with all her heart that her mum and dad could have been there.

What would they have felt to see their daughter marry a Palvetti? She wished she knew but all she had were the memories formed as a child which, though she had tried desperately to remember them, had faded through the years.

The burn of Palvetti stares scorched her skin and she held tightly to Alessio's huge hand as they approached the desk with the waiting officiant.

Forcing an image of Dom into her mind, she finally managed to get air into her lungs.

Dom was the reason she was taking this step. If she ran out now, she would be cut from his life.

Under a gleaming chandelier they exchanged their vows, Alessio's voice strong, hers not much above a whisper, and signed the document that legally bound her to his side for the rest of her life.

Silence filled the great room.

The officiant had not said the immortal words but she could taste the anticipation of the many witnesses and knew they were waiting for the kiss that would seal the deal.

And then she met Alessio's gaze and her heart skipped.

Dressed in a black dinner jacket and bow-tie, he was more devilishly handsome than ever.

That gleam she was coming to know so well shone from the emeralds and contained more brilliance than any polished chandelier.

Her veins heated.

Hands cupped her flaming cheeks.

The handsome face that had hovered in her mind for so long inched closer to hers. The sensuous mouth her lips had tingled with such fervour to kiss…

Her trembling lips tingled now.

She struggled to breathe again but this felt different from the closed lungs of fear that had accompanied her down the aisle, more of a tight quickening.

His dark, sweeping lashes flashed before her and then the mouth she had dreamed about covered hers and his scent filled her.

Heat rushed through her every crevice and suddenly she was taken back to her dream of them together, in her bed…

He'd been making love to her.

The sticky heat flowing through her now was the heat she'd woken up with then.

The chaste kiss could only have lasted a few seconds but in that heady moment time came to a standstill.

And then he broke away and moved his hands from her face to lace them in her fingers.

She stared at him, dazed, not so much at the kiss but at the maelstrom of feelings that had erupted from it.

It felt as if there were something beating within her heart thrashing to escape.

Beth stepped into what was already her old bedroom. All her stuff had been taken out. It was as if she had never been there.

The nursery, however, was exactly as she had left it that morning.

She crept to the cot. The tooth that had caused Dom such pain had come through that morning and now he slept peacefully.

Miranda was in her adjoining room, the television playing low.

Beth brushed Dom's forehead lightly with her fingers and blew him a goodnight kiss.

Treading slowly up the corridor, her stomach twisting with nerves, she reached Alessio's room.

She sent a silent prayer for courage then knocked.

'Come in.'

Another quick prayer and then she opened it.

Even with all the turmoil knotting so tightly within her, she experienced a moment of pure princess's delight to see the interior of his room.

A vast marble floor reflected the colours of the deep maroon of the walls and heavy curtains, with flecks of gold mirroring off the gold pillars encircling the room and gold architrave, and the large crystal and gold chandelier hanging from the ceiling. A gold and dark brown leather bed even larger than the one she'd been sleeping in stood at the far end of the room atop a sumptuous, obviously expensive thick rug.

But it was to the man standing at the dresser below one of the windows, casually removing his cufflinks, that her gaze was drawn.

The soft lighting in the room seemed to magnify him.

He stared at her. 'There is no need to knock,

bella. This is your bedroom now. Make yourself at home. Drink?'

He put his cufflinks on the dresser and reached for a bottle of Scotch at the back of it.

'You drink in your bedroom?'

White teeth flashed briefly. 'Not as a rule but I thought you would be in need of it. I know today has not been easy for you.'

She leant against the wall, touched at this small display of empathy.

He'd surprised her with little touches of it throughout the day.

The Palvettis had come to the villa after the ceremony for a champagne reception and, as she'd been introduced to them, she'd understood why Domenico had loathed them so much. Some actually seemed quite nice but a hard-core group's verbal welcomes had been matched with cold eyes, their welcoming kisses to her cheeks perfunctory. If Alessio hadn't stuck to her side like glue she would probably have hidden in the nursery.

They were so assured and sophisticated. Beside their glossy polish she'd felt drab and inadequate. She could only hope the apathy she

sensed from them was her imagination working overtime.

Alessio's father and much of the older generation of Palvettis had been wonderful, though.
She'd been amazed at his father's friendliness
and the way he'd fussed over Dom. Bruno and
his brother, who she'd learned was the infa-
mous divorcé Giuseppe, had been the last to
leave. They'd consumed more champagne than
everyone else put together and had staggered
out of the villa in high spirits.

'Your father's really nice.'

'You are surprised?' He poured them both a
large measure.

'I suppose I am,' she admitted.

He carried the glasses over and held one out
to her. 'Because of what my brother told you
about us?'

She took the glass from him. Tingles ran
through her fingers when he brushed his against
hers. 'I'm beginning to accept that some of the
things he told me were…' She didn't want to
say 'downright lies'.

'Variations and degrees of truth?' he sup-
plied.

She nodded with a grimace. Beth had taken

everything Domenico had said at face value, but now she needed to judge the Palvettis for herself, and that meant doing as Alessio had asked last night and giving him—and by extension his family—the benefit of the doubt.

'In my experience, it is a person's actions that count, not their words.' He took a large drink of his Scotch, his emerald gaze staying on hers. 'But I don't want to talk about my brother. This is our wedding night.'

Her heart thudded as he took the one step needed to gently cup her cheek.

'You take my breath away, *bella*.' Then he brought his face to hers and captured her mouth in a kiss that was even more fleeting than the one he'd given her to seal their marriage.

But it stole her breath even more than that first one had.

'I'm going to take a shower,' he murmured into her ear. 'You have your own bathroom—it's through the door behind you. The door inside it opens to your dressing room.'

He traced his finger down her cheek then stepped back, downed his Scotch and strolled to the door on the other side of the vast bedroom, placing his empty glass on the bureau as he went.

Beth caught a glimpse of a palatial bathroom before the door closed behind him.

She blew out the lungful of air she'd hardly been aware she was holding then tipped the rest of her drink into her mouth. It was such a large swallow the fiery liquid almost choked her.

Her eyes were still watering when she walked into her own bathroom.

She blinked rapidly as she took in the sumptuousness of it.

From the glimpse she'd seen of Alessio's private bathroom, hers matched it in all ways.

Beth had hosted events in five-star hotels before. This bathroom made those ones feel like two stars.

Her dressing room was similarly sized. All the clothes and accessories she'd bought on her shopping trip had been neatly put away and filled barely a tenth of the available space.

Her hands shook as she selected a nightshirt to wear and shook even harder to know it wouldn't stay on her for any length of time.

She needed to tell him.

She dragged her shower out as long as she could but it seemed no time had passed before she stood in front of the mirror, nightshirt and fresh knickers on, teeth and hair brushed.

She stared at her reflection and prayed for courage.

So many emotions were skittling through her, she could hardly differentiate between them. Fear, excitement, nausea, all there churning inside her.

Her head pounded. Her heart did too. She *had* to tell him.

It took another minute before she could get her feet to walk to the door. She held her breath as she unlocked it and pushed it open an inch. The gap wasn't wide enough for her to see the bed. She pushed it a little more and put her eye to the crack.

Alessio was sat upright in the bed.

Her toes ground to the floor and she rocked on her heels while trying to lower the rate of her accelerating heartbeat.

The last time she'd been this scared was when she thought he'd stolen Dom from her.

But this was a different kind of fear. Huge butterflies of anticipation were laced with it too.

She counted to ten, took a deep breath, then pushed the door open.

CHAPTER EIGHT

BETH'S INTENTION TO blurt out her virgin state dissolved when she took the first step into the bedroom and looked at Alessio.

While she'd been in the bathroom he'd turned off all the lights except for the one above the bed. It cast him in a golden halo, magnifying him so he was the only defined thing in the room.

Legs trembling, she forced her feet towards him. Heat flushed her cheeks, the blush sliding its way down her body and into her veins as he became clearer in her vision.

His deep olive skin was smooth and unblemished, the muscles of his chest and biceps more defined than she'd imagined. Fine dark hair nestled lightly between his pecs, a thin line of thicker hair running to his navel, where it thickened again...

The satin sheets covered what lay beneath that...

Her heart set into a canter. The heavy beats echoed through skin that suddenly felt tight and sticky.

If there was a word to describe rampant male sexuality that word was Alessio.

She did not think she had ever felt so scared. Or so...

Charged. It was as if she had an electric current running through the cells of her body and the charge from it terrified her as much as the expectations of the man waiting on the bed did.

When she reached the bed, she turned back the covers on her side, climbed in and lay on her back beside him.

He lowered himself down, propped his head on his hand and gazed at her.

The look in his eyes...

It was the look of hunger. And she was the food he intended to feast on.

She tried to breathe. She tried to speak. She could do neither. All she could do was stare into the swirling emerald, trapped in his gaze and trapped in a body paralysed with fear and anticipation.

His face came closer to hers. His warm breath whispered over her cheek.

He put a finger to her shoulder and gently brushed it over her collarbone to the top button of her nightshirt. He undid it.

His finger skimmed her skin before moving onto the next two buttons and suddenly she was filled with a new sensation, one that fought the fear, a furnace growing in her veins that melted into her bones.

Not a word was exchanged as he continued on his quest. Her heart beat so fast it was nothing but a heavy blur compressing in her.

And then he separated the nightshirt, first one side then the other, exposing her to him.

The dizzying sensations were abruptly driven away.

Alessio sucked in a sharp breath and closed his eyes to gather himself. But only for a moment. Beth was too exquisite to shut away from his vision.

He'd anticipated this moment from that first meeting between them all those weeks ago.

She'd strolled into that boardroom in London with that beautiful smile and he'd felt something move inside him. That something had been with him ever since, an itch he'd been unable to scratch…until tonight.

He pressed his nose to her hair and breathed in the scent that evoked thoughts of marshmallows, then moved his hand lower to stroke her belly. He'd never imagined skin could be so soft to the touch.

She was exquisite.

Her breasts were fuller than he'd imagined and a lighter tone than the rest of her. They rose and fell with the raggedness of her breaths.

Inching his face closer to hers, he circled a taut cherry-red nipple with his finger.

She inhaled sharply.

He drifted his gaze back up to meet her eyes. They were wide on his…

He brought his face down to capture the full lips with his own. Heat filled him at the pliant softness he found.

He felt another sharp inhalation before she responded with the utmost tentativeness.

The hands his body ached to feel on his skin stayed by her sides.

He shifted slightly, moving his mouth from hers and brushing it over her cheeks, then over her nose and eyes, light caresses from his lips while his hands explored, running over the plane of her stomach and down to the only part of her still covered.

When he threaded a finger beneath the band of her knickers, she jerked, clamped her thighs together and twisted her hips away from him.

He opened his eyes to see her hands were clenched into fists and her eyes squeezed shut.

It took a moment to register what he was seeing and, when it did, it was like having a spray of cold water hosed over him.

His desire extinguished in an instant.

He moved abruptly off her, threw the covers back and climbed off the bed.

'What game are you playing?' Alessio's deep voice cut through Beth's ringing ears.

It took real effort to open her eyes.

He stood some distance from the bed, fully, unashamedly, terrifyingly naked.

She scrambled upright, drawing her nightshirt together to hide her own nakedness.

'*Is* this a game?' His brows drew together in confusion. 'Or have I got everything wrong?'

She swallowed, trying to get her frozen throat to work, but failing miserably.

Beth had long been aware of her desire for Alessio but *nothing* could have prepared her for the sensations that had erupted. She'd been sinking into it, had been falling into a heady state where her mind had almost closed itself off...

But then he'd pulled her nightshirt apart.

His face contorted. 'Do not play me for a fool. If you don't want me, then have the guts to admit it, but do not just lie there as if my touch is something to be endured.' And with that he paced to his bathroom and slammed the door behind him.

Beth sagged and clutched at her head, fighting for air.

Like everything else in this new life of hers, the feelings evoked by Alessio's touch overwhelmed her.

She quickly fastened one of the buttons on her nightshirt with fumbling fingers.

No one had seen her breasts before let alone touched them.

It had felt...

God, it had felt wonderful. But it had been excruciating. She'd been painfully aware of the soft light above them shining on her, revealing all her imperfections.

Beth wasn't polished and preened to within

an inch of her life like his other lovers would have been, and when he had reached down to touch her in that most intimate place panic had taken control and now she'd ruined everything.

The bathroom door flew back open and Alessio reappeared with a pair of unbuttoned jeans on. Not looking at her, he strode to the bedroom door.

A different kind of panic filled her.

'Don't go,' she croaked before he could slam that door too.

He stilled, his fingers clasped on the handle, his cold back to her. 'Why not?'

'Please… Can't we just…talk?'

He slowly faced her. Deep suspicion was etched on his face. 'You want to *talk*?'

She nodded and bit her lip.

'Talk about what?'

Oh, God, how could she find the words to explain herself when she'd never found them before? Alessio was such a rampantly sexy man, he would never understand why this was such a big deal to her. *She'd* never realised what a big deal it was either.

'Why don't you start with telling me why you've been giving me come-to-bed eyes since we met and now that we are here, on our wedding night, you reject me.'

'I didn't...'

His laugh was short and bitter. 'Not in words. You didn't need words. Your body spoke for you. What did you think? That you *had* to give yourself to me? Did you think I would annul our marriage if it wasn't consummated?'

She shook her head while red-hot flames engulfed her face and burned through her brain.

'Trust me, *bella*, I would rather live like a monk than have sex with an unwilling woman.'

'I'm not unwilling. I'm... It's just...' She covered her face with her hands. 'It's just... I've never done this before.'

There was a long pause. 'Done what?'

'This. Sex.'

Alessio stared at Beth, her knees drawn to her chest, her face hidden by her hands, disbelief rising in him. 'You're a virgin?'

The silence that carried through the bedroom was the starkest he had ever known.

It took an age before she pulled her hands from her face to meet his eyes.

If he'd thought she was lying, the bleakness of her stare spoke the truth.

She nodded.

'How?'

Her shoulders hunched even further.

Legs suddenly feeling like weights had been placed in them, he stepped to the bed and carefully sat beside her, being sure to keep his feet on the floor.

'I'm sorry,' she whispered.

'I have no idea what you're apologising for,' he said heavily.

'This. Here. Tonight. It isn't that I don't want you...' Her voice trailed off before she whispered, 'I got scared.'

'Of me?'

'I haven't kissed a man since I was eighteen and that's the furthest I've gone.'

The weight in his legs moved up to lodge in his chest and he raised his head to stare at the ceiling. Nothing but a kiss since she was eighteen?

'No wonder you got scared,' he muttered.

What had stopped her? Beth was beautiful. She would have had an army of men beating down her door.

He felt her eyes on him. 'I panicked. I know

you've been with lots of women before but I've never been naked in front of anyone.'

'Beth…' Alessio rubbed his hair and tried to gather his scattered thoughts. 'I wish you'd told me.'

'I should have done but I didn't know how.' Her voice dropped even lower. 'The only time we've spent alone together since you brought me here was last night on the bridge when you told me you'd had other women lined up to marry.'

He turned his head to meet her forlorn gaze. His heart made a painful thump against his ribs.

He remembered reading the investigator's report on her and the relief that had swept through him to read the words that there was no evidence Beth had a current lover.

He would never have guessed the bright, confident woman who had shone in that first meeting had never had *any* lover.

He imagined his nonchalance about other women had only added to her insecurity and could have kicked himself for telling her about them.

Beth was not of his world. She had yet to

learn how to see things from a Palvetti perspective or learn to detach her emotions. He'd brought her into this world. It was down to him to teach her.

'You know the reasons why I chose you to marry.' He rested a hand against her cheek and stroked it gently. 'Those reasons haven't changed and nor have my thoughts. I have never wanted a woman the way I want you. Those other women…they were just thoughts. I never pursued them and never desired them. But you… I would have wanted you even if I hadn't been planning to marry you.'

Her chest rose. The colour that stained her face was a lighter hue than the mortification that had been rent across it a few minutes earlier.

He pressed his lips to her and breathed her in, then nuzzled his nose against her cheek, capturing that scent of marshmallow again. 'You're my wife. I married you for life. There's no pressure, *bella*. I can wait. We will not make love until you're ready.'

She stared at him for the longest time before whispering, 'I *am* ready.'

He brushed another gentle kiss to her then

pulled away, knowing to keep touching her was dangerous. 'No, you're not. You don't owe me sex.'

Beth thought her heart could burst.

Never in her wildest dreams had she imagined Alessio Palvetti could be so selfless. And understanding.

The fear that had clawed at her melted away.

Now she was the one to reach for him, placing her hands on his cheeks and forcing him to look at her. It was the first time she had touched him and she marvelled at the texture of his skin, the same yet somehow different from hers. The bristles of his stubble rubbed against her hand.

Staring deep into his eyes, she said quietly, 'I do want you, Alessio. The things you make me feel when you touch me are like nothing I've felt before.'

She spoke only the truth. She *did* want him. She'd wanted him from the first moment she'd set eyes on him.

That dream she'd had of them together had set something off in her and suddenly she knew she wanted to feel what she'd felt then for real.

No more waiting. No more sick fear.

Heart hammering, she brushed her lips lightly to his.

He reared back and grabbed at the hands holding his cheeks. 'Beth…' Her name came out as groan.

She pressed the tips of her fingers to his cheeks. 'Everything you made me feel was so new and…so *much* that I panicked. I don't want to be scared any more. I don't want to wait.'

He breathed heavily, his jaw taut.

She could see the anguish of his internal battle in his eyes and her heart expanded all the more for it.

'I made this commitment to *you*, Alessio. I want our wedding night.'

There was a long moment when neither of them spoke, when his eyes did nothing but bore into hers, as if he were trying to read her thoughts.

And then the tightness of his jaw loosened and his mouth closed on hers in a kiss of such tenderness she could have cried. His hand touched her shoulder, gently moved across her back and then up to cradle her head.

And then he splayed his fingers in her hair and parted her lips with his.

Everything inside her bloomed.

Beth closed her eyes and sank into it, letting her senses run free to savour the dark heat of his breath and the firmness of the lips that had taken control and were manipulating hers. Every nerve ending tingled.

When she felt the first dart of his tongue against hers, a bolt of sensation crashed through her.

But there was no accompanying panic.

He kissed her for an age in a slow, deep, sensual fusion, then slowly laid her down.

'Any time you want me to stop, tell me.'

She stared into the emerald eyes, hooded and dark, her heart thumping too hard and too near her throat for words to form.

All she could do was touch his face.

Her breath quickened.

When he brought his head down to claim her in another deep kiss, the warmth that flooded through her had her looping her arms around his neck and lifting her chest to press against his.

She could have cried when he pulled away and stepped off the bed, but the tears would only have turned into gasps, for he hooked his hands on his jeans and pushed them down.

He was already fully aroused. It was a sight that filled her with thick warmth and made her pelvis tighten and pulse.

She couldn't tear her gaze from him, the man who had deceived her and blackmailed her into a marriage and a life she didn't want, yet who had awoken something feminine and primitive in her. A man who, she was learning, was capable of empathy and tenderness.

Domenico had been wrong about him, she thought dimly as she watched Alessio kick his jeans away, but then the rest of her thoughts slipped away as he lay back down on his side beside her.

She put her hand to his jaw and rubbed her palm against the stubble. There was something about the way the bristles felt against her skin...

He skimmed a hand across her chest to the one closed button. He undid it then, like the last time, parted the shirt, first one side, then the other.

Her fingers clutched at his cheek and she inhaled deeply through her nose, keeping her eyes on his, taking strength from the desire swirling back at her.

Her nightshirt was slowly peeled off her body and discarded, then new heated sensation danced over her skin as he ran his hand between her cleavage and over her stomach to rest on the band of her knickers.

Beth swallowed back the automatic panic rising up her throat and slowly raised her abdomen, lifting her bottom from the mattress so he could tug her knickers down.

His eyes still didn't leave her face, not even when he pulled the knickers over her feet and threw them onto the floor.

Not until he'd kissed her again and laced his fingers through hers did his eyes move from her face to drift over her body.

She was certain he must be able to see her heart beating like a giant hummingbird's wings beneath her chest.

Alessio took in every inch of Beth's beautiful body with that one long look.

There was not one inch of her that didn't make his loins sing and tighten way past the point he'd ever considered endurable.

The times he'd imagined this moment…

He'd imagined himself devouring her whole.

He'd imagined a tangle of limbs and a frenzy of urgency.

He'd never imagined she was a virgin.

But he would have guessed at her inexperience, he thought thickly, seeing the way she subconsciously pressed her thighs together when he cast his gaze over her soft, downy womanhood and the colour that crept over her face when he looked back into her eyes.

There was a shyness in her returning stare but no fear.

That she would trust *him* of all people with this, the most precious gift a woman could give a man...

It made his heart swell so hard that, without his ribs to contain it, it would have burst out of him.

He placed a hand flat on her shoulder then slowly drew it down her. Her throat moved and he felt her body quiver. When he reached her breasts, her fingers squeezed against his and her breaths shortened.

His breath shortened too.

He'd never in his whole life been as aware of his arousal as he was then. It was more than a mere concentration in his loins. It lived in him. It breathed through his skin, lifting all the hairs on his body, and tingled on the pads of the palm and fingers exploring her beautiful body.

She nestled her face closer to his, her shining eyes staring straight into his.

He drew his hand lower, over her belly then down to her hips and thighs, watching her expressive eyes' responses to his touches.

And then he drew it all the way back up to capture her chin and bring his face down for another kiss.

Her response was full of such passion and hunger that if he hadn't such a tight handle on his own raging arousal he would have rolled on top of her, spread her legs and thrust straight into her.

Instead, he kept his ardour in check and explored her body anew, this time with his mouth as well as his fingers.

Dio, her golden skin had that same marshmallow scent of her hair.

When he closed his mouth over a puckered cherry nipple, she writhed beneath him and moaned.

The taste of her skin was its own aphrodisiac.

As he moved lower, kissing every part of her belly, he marvelled at the soft yet jagged moans and the hands that followed his movements so she was always touching him…and then he tasted the musky, heated scent of her excitement…

Beth was floating on a cloud.

It felt as if Alessio had shrouded her in a cocoon of bliss, her body awakening to new pleasures that sent her senses soaring.

His touch…

When he'd kissed her right in the heart of her own swollen arousal…

His tenderness had stopped any shyness she would have expected to feel at this most intimate experience and she closed her eyes and melted into it.

The pulse that had throbbed low inside her since he had brushed his lips against hers for the first time had grown. The feeling she was on the crest of something magical thrummed through her like a low buzz dancing through her cells.

But, just as she found herself reaching the peak of the crest she was climbing, he moved his mouth away.

The disappointment was fleeting.

He kissed his way back up in another sensory explosion before finding her mouth. His chest crushed against the hyper-sensitive skin of her breasts as their tongues tangled together and a new taste played on her senses...

That was *her* taste, mingled with the dark taste of Alessio, and when she wrapped her arms around his neck she became aware of even more: the musky heat of his skin...the *feel* of his skin, warmth flushing and pulsing in her pelvis, and...

A heavy weight pressed against the top of her inner thigh that she realised with a thud of her heart was the weight of his arousal.

He pulled his mouth away and raised his head to look down at her.

The hunger she'd felt in his touch and kisses reflected in the swirling emerald.

His next kiss was almost chaste.

He shifted, only a touch, but enough to part her thighs a little more and for his arousal to...

She swallowed, suddenly frightened of the thick, heavy weight pushing against her.

As if he sensed her fear, Alessio placed his hands either side of her head and gently stroked his fingers through her hair. His mouth found hers again, a long, lingering brush of his lips on hers.

The fear left as suddenly as it had arrived and she tightened her hold around him.

His hips moved and the weight pushing against her increased.

His mouth moved to rain kisses over her cheeks.

His arousal pushed in a little further.

'I've got you, *bella*,' he whispered into her ear.

Slowly, gently, he rocked into her, bit by bit, inch by inch, kissing her and stroking her, relaxing her into his love-making so thoroughly that by the time he was fully inside her she opened her eyes with astonishment at the incredible feelings suddenly filling her.

He filled her.

Dear God, Alessio was inside her, a part of her, and...

Staring straight back at her.

Eyes locked on hers, he began to move.

Sensation she could never have imagined whirled into life.

He made love to her with a tenderness she

could never have imagined. She knew he was holding back, that all of this was for her virgin pleasure, and her heart bloomed all over again for him.

The cocoon of bliss shrouded her again and lifted her back to the clouds. She clung to Alessio, taking him with her as she soared high, climbing the crest, higher and higher until she found herself flying into a world of bright lights and stardust as the pleasure finally found its peak and erupted through her.

It took a long time for her to drift back to earth and when she did she found herself on another cloud.

If she climbed off this bed now she wouldn't be surprised to find only air beneath her feet.

CHAPTER NINE

ALESSIO WAS SLUMPED on top of her, breathing heavily into her neck, his skin damp with perspiration.

She kissed his ear.

He mumbled something and raised his head.

Beth read the question in his eyes and, with a smile, palmed his cheek.

He kissed her gently then rolled off her onto his back.

The sudden chill on her skin at the removal of his heat made her shiver but before she could feel the cold too much he tugged at the sheets and brought them up to cover them both. She turned on her side to face him.

Alessio reached out to turn the light off.

The instant darkness was welcome.

He felt exposed in a way he'd never experienced before.

He'd been so intent on making sure it was good for Beth that it wasn't until now, that it was over, that he could appreciate how mind-blowing it had been for him.

He could still feel the thrills of his release in his loins, on his skin and in the thuds of his heart. There was a weight in his limbs but for once there was no immediate lethargy in his brain.

What he had felt in her arms…it had been more than physical. It had been something else. It was this unidentifiable something else that must account for the feeling of exposure.

But, however out of kilter and exposed he felt, he could not feel as exposed as Beth must.

He shifted onto his side to face her. His vision had adjusted enough to the darkness to see her eyes were open and on him.

He captured a lock of her silky hair. 'Did I hurt you?'

The tip of her nose rubbed against his. 'No.'

'Any regrets?'

'None. If anything, I feel relief.'

'Relief?'

Beth thought of what she should say to explain what she was feeling without making herself sound weak.

She'd seen enough of the world to know men thought of sex differently from women.

Making love to Alessio…

It had been wonderful. Better than she could have dreamed. Better than she *had* dreamed. But he had enough power in their marriage without him knowing how deeply moved the whole experience had left her.

She settled on, 'I think I built it up in my mind to be this big, terrifying thing and now I don't have to be scared any more. It's done.'

There was a long pause before he asked, 'Why did you wait so long?'

'It wasn't intentional.'

When he didn't fill the silence, she felt compelled to explain, although she knew even as she started to speak that this was only a partial truth. 'I was an eighteen-year-old virgin when I moved to London and started working at White's Events, and pretty sheltered about the more debauched ways of the world. My eyes were opened quickly. We hosted parties and events of all shapes and sizes where the one constant was that alcohol was always on tap. Lots of the guests assumed event staff were up for it…many *were* up for it.'

'But not you.'

'No way.' She made sure to inject brightness as she spoke, not wanting Alessio to think there was anything more than the tale she was narrating. 'I didn't want my first time to be a notch on some drunken idiot's bed post and dumped the next morning. My life was busy. I had a great career, a fun social life… The longer I was single, the choosier I became. I knew what I didn't want in a man but I never found what I did want.'

'What did you want?'

Someone to love.

'Someone who would respect me.' A sudden burn of tears filled the back of her eyes.

All she'd wanted since her parents had died was to know that in this world there was one person who loved her. She'd found a version of that with Caroline but that had been a love of friendship and sisterhood built on mutual grief, two castaways clinging together. As she'd matured, she'd longed for emotional intimacy but, she could see now, had shied away from it too, scared of love that could be lost at the turn of fortune's wheel.

She blinked back the tears, thankful the darkness stopped Alessio seeing them, and injected brightness into her voice. 'Now that the noose of my virginity has gone, it feels like a weight's been lifted from me. It's the same with our wedding—I was terrified in the run-up to it but, now that it's done, it's done.'

He propped himself on an elbow and traced a finger down her cheek.

She shivered and swallowed to contain a rush of emotion that suddenly had her yearn to wrap her arms around him and cling tightly to his strength.

Alessio might have displayed a tenderness and empathy she would never have thought him capable of but he would not want that. Palvetti wives could be many things but emotional was not one of them.

He placed a lingering kiss to her lips and murmured, 'And, now that "it's done", how do you feel about doing it again?'

Her heart expanded so hard it filled her chest.

Love might never be a part of their marriage but she would have this.

And, as she embraced his love-making a second time, she thought that, if this was all the intimacy she would have from their marriage, that would be enough.

It would have to be.

'You look pale,' Alessio observed the next morning when Beth joined him for breakfast. 'Are you feeling all right?'

'I'm fine,' she said with a brittle smile. 'Do I look okay?'

He looked her up and down and marvelled to see the colour rise up her face. That she could still blush after the night they'd just shared...

'You look beautiful.' So beautiful that if they didn't have to leave for work shortly he would have carried her up the stairs and made love to her again.

'What about my clothes?'

She'd dressed conservatively but fashionably in a form-fitting high-necked navy dress that fell to her knees and a pair of black heels. She'd left her hair loose, spilling over her shoulders. His fingers itched to touch it.

'It's not a fashion parade.'

She took the seat opposite him. 'I know that but I don't want to stick out.'

'You're my wife.' He experienced a real surge

of satisfaction calling her that. 'You're going to stick out.'

She rolled her eyes and poured herself a coffee. 'Thanks for the comfort. What will I be doing when we get there?'

'Today, tomorrow and next week, you will shadow me. You will accompany me to meetings and read the files for each department so you can become familiar with everything.'

'And then what?'

'And then you will start shadowing the other directors.'

'How many are there?'

He noticed she added two extra spoons of sugar than normal.

'Four of us in total. Once you have shadowed all of us, we will sit down and discuss which area you are best suited for.'

'What if you don't think I'm suited for anything?'

'You will be.'

'But what if I'm not? And what if your family all hate me or find me wanting?'

He reached over the table to cover the hand still absently stirring the sugar.

Memories of her white-faced fear before

the wedding surfaced, along with her terrified nerves before they'd made love. His mind pushed back further to remember her agitation on their drive to the palace when her nerves about getting everything right for the masquerade ball had rippled from her.

He had no doubt her current nerves would disappear as soon as she started working. If he'd learned anything about Beth it was that once she'd confronted her fears they were put to bed as if they'd never existed in the first place. It was the build-up to confronting them that was the challenge.

'Why do you always think the worst of situations?' he asked, curious to understand more about his wife.

'I don't. I just like to prepare myself for worst-case scenarios.'

'It's the same thing.'

'Not really. I always hope for the best.' And then she gave a burst of shaky laughter. 'God, I thought having sex for the first time was scary.'

Their eyes met and held. He could almost see the same images flashing through her mind as were in his: locked lips, entwined limbs, perspiration glistening on them both…

Willing away the tightening in his limbs the images provoked, Alessio cleared his throat.

Soon they would leave for work. Beth was going to be introduced to the most important part of his world. Fantasising about carrying her up the stairs...

He pushed his chair back. 'Eat something, *bella*,' he ordered gently. 'It will settle your stomach. We leave in ten minutes.'

The closeness and joy Beth had found in Alessio's arms on their wedding night solidified her intention to make the best of her situation. She went to work with him that first day filled with nerves but determined to find a role within Palvetti as fulfilling as she'd found at White's Events.

Palvetti was synonymous with sophistication and glamour. How could she fail to find something she enjoyed?

Quite easily, as it transpired.

Exactly two weeks after starting there, the only thing she enjoyed about it was the building they worked from.

Set in the heart of the fashion district, the sixteenth-century building that housed the

Palvetti administrative headquarters looked so much like the others in the vicinity that no one would look twice at it in passing. Recent major renovations had created a vast network of functional offices and creative studios, and yet despite the efficiency that breathed through the walls there was an air of romance to it too, almost as if the elusive brand the family had created had seeped into the building's core. It evoked her imagination.

She wished the work she'd been given evoked it too. She wished the thick files of accounts Gina had dumped on the desk of the tiny box room she'd shoved Beth into didn't give her a headache. But they did.

She was sat in that excuse for an office when Alessio walked in.

She brightened to see him. It was the first time he'd visited her since she'd started shadowing Gina four days ago.

She'd actually enjoyed the days she'd spent shadowing him. He'd put her in a decent-sized, airy office that adjoined his own and kept the dividing door open so he was always on hand for any questions she had. All she'd done while shadowing him was read through documents and files to familiarise herself with the different aspects and territories of the business, but she'd never felt unwanted. He'd eased her in gently. Working for his cousin Gina...

Not only did Beth have zero interest in finance but Gina was easily the least welcoming of the Palvettis. An immaculately dressed stocky woman, with platinum hair that managed to be classy rather than brassy, when Gina had embraced Beth at their wedding reception it had been like being hugged by an iceberg.

It was a coldness that showed no sign of abating.

'I've got a meeting at the production facility,' Alessio told her, nothing on his face to suggest he'd woken her with his love-making before the sun had risen.

For all the passion that took them when the bedroom door was closed, the only thing that consumed Alessio's attention in the waking hours was the business.

His detachment outside the bedroom had to be innate. And why it even bothered her she didn't know. This was nothing she hadn't expected. It was her own feelings that should trouble her, not his.

She shouldn't long for him. Alessio had been explicit about the marriage he wanted and that was the marriage she'd signed up for.

'I've arranged for a driver to take you home if I'm not back by five.'

Although Beth welcomed the early finish, she thought longingly of the production facility, known informally as the workshop.

The workshop was the beating heart of Palvetti, the place in which all their exquisite jewellery was designed and created. The scents and cosmetics they produced in their laboratories were a high-value tie-in to it, a concept sold to the rich as the ultimate badge of wealth, but a badge that should be kept secret and elusive.

Everything about Palvetti was secret and elusive.

And so far she'd been privy only to their most minor secrets. She had no idea where the workshop was located. She longed to visit it and see for herself how their beautiful creations came into being.

'Can I come with you?'

The emerald eyes held hers for a beat before he shook his head. 'I'm going with Marcello.'

Marcello was Gina's husband and the Palvetti creative director.

'Okay.' She tried to hide her disappointment with a smile.

But it wasn't just disappointment at not being allowed to go to the workshop with him. She hated when he left headquarters without her. Even though she hadn't seen much of him during business hours this week, knowing Alessio was just a few doors up the corridor had given her a small modicum of comfort when dealing with Gina's iciness.

Alessio put his hands on her desk and studied his wife closely. 'Are you?'

'What?'

'Okay? Is something the matter?'

She shrugged, no longer meeting his eyes.

'Beth?'

She rubbed her forehead. In a small voice, she admitted, 'I'm struggling.'

'With finance?'

'It might as well be in Latin for all I understand of it. I'm used to working under set budgets for events and that's fine, I manage okay with them, but anything else to do with finance...'

To his shock, Alessio saw a shimmer in Beth's eyes.

She was holding back tears.

The urge to take her in his arms was strong.

He cursed inwardly.

The first two weeks of their marriage had gone much better than he could have hoped. Beth had accompanied him to the office every business day. When she'd shadowed him, she'd read the thick files he'd given her diligently, had asked pertinent questions, been pleasant with the lower-ranking staff and generally an all-round good presence. The evenings...

He drove away thoughts of the long, hot nights they shared.

Fantasies were not a luxury he allowed himself in the workplace but, *Dio*, it had been hard to keep his head where it should be when all he'd had to do was glance through the opened adjoining door and see his wife with her head bowed in concentration and imagine it in a far more intimate place.

That was one thing he hadn't expected—that Beth's presence would be such a distraction. He'd never imagined he would be on the phone with a client wishing to purchase over five million euros of jewellery on a special commission and would lose his train of thought because his wife had dropped something off her desk and leaned over to pick it up, giving him a brief glimpse of golden, creamy cleavage.

It had been a relief to go in that Monday and have her move to be under Gina's tutelage. No more distractions…

Until he'd found himself having to fight his thoughts away from her.

He'd resisted visiting her in Gina's domain until now.

He looked grimly around the windowless cubby-hole his cousin had stuck his wife in and wondered if this had something to do with Beth's low mood.

'Tell me what you're thinking,' he commanded gently. 'I can't help you if you won't talk to me.'

'It's nothing specific,' she answered in a small voice. 'It's just so different from my old job. I'm just finding things a bit overwhelming, that's all.'

'And Gina?'

Immediately her expression became wary. 'What about her?'

'How are you finding working with her?'

Her shoulders rose as she bit her lip. Then she blurted out, 'She hates me.'

'What's she done to make you feel that?'

'Nothing specific. Maybe I'm being over-sensitive, but she never looks at me when she's talking to me, and when I attend meetings with her she makes me feel like an unwanted stray dog she's been saddled with. I get the same vibes from the other directors.'

'Gina's a hard woman but once she gets to know you and realises she can trust you you'll find her a good friend.'

In the meantime, Alessio thought grimly, he was going to bang some heads together. He'd told his family—the directors specifically—to treat Beth with respect.

'Trust me?' she asked with a crease in her brow.

'They don't trust you yet,' he admitted.

Her face fell. 'Why?'

'Because you were Domenico's friend. Domenico hated us. They worry you are planning to destroy us from within.'

'That's ridiculous.'

'I know.'

'Do you?'

He leaned forward. 'Yes.'

Beth had committed to their marriage in body and in spirit. No one knew that better than him.

'Is that why you've not taken me to the workshop?'

'Yes.'

Her eyes held his before she sighed. 'Thank you for being honest.'

'We will find something you enjoy,' he told her. His mind raced as he thought of what that something could be. Their marketing was subtle and under the radar. Unless you knew what you were looking for you wouldn't see it. They did not throw the kind of events and parties Beth had run. 'I need to go. Marcello's waiting for me. You should go too—take the rest of the day off. Get some distance from the office. Find a new perspective on things.'

Her brow creased. 'Really? Won't Gina mind?'

'Don't worry about Gina. I will deal with things. *Va bene?*'

She nodded.

'And Beth?'

'Yes?'

'Next time something's troubling you, come to me. I can't help you if I don't know.'

Her smile made his heart clench.

'Before I forget, we're going out Saturday night.'

Beth's deflated spirits lifted. 'Great. Where are we going?'

'It's a business dinner.'

A business dinner on a Saturday night?

Her spirits fell flat as quickly as they'd lifted. For a few wonderful seconds she'd thought her husband was going to take her out on a proper date.

In this respect at least, Domenico had been right about his family. They were workaholics. Their lives revolved around the business, with early starts and late finishes the norm.

Alessio even worked weekends. Thankfully he hadn't expected her to go to the office with him, or even suggested it, for which she was grateful, just as she was grateful he hadn't dismissed her concerns out of hand and was grateful for this unexpected early finish which would give her some precious time with Dom.

She thought wistfully of the Saturday nights of old, before Caroline's diagnosis, when Beth had had an evening off work. Nights out watching live music, dancing, drinking more than was sensible, tottering back to her small flat with friends in tow to carry on partying. Dancing in her living room. Enjoying life. Aware that every moment was precious and that it could all end in a heartbeat.

He must have seen her disappointment for he smiled ruefully. 'It will be good for you. It's with our Chinese representative. He confirmed a few minutes ago.'

She forced her own smile. 'I'll look forward to it.'

CHAPTER TEN

BETH'S EARLY FINISH and the unexpected extra hours she got with Dom went all too quickly. In no time, the morning arrived and she was kissing her baby goodbye and heading for the car, all over again.

'You look sad,' Alessio commented as their driver bullied his way out of their estate and into the Milanese traffic.

'I just hate knowing I won't be home before Dom goes to bed.' She attempted a smile. Having been home in time to feed Dom his dinner, bathe him and put him to bed on a work day for the first time since the wedding had only served to remind her how badly she missed being with him. 'I'm sure I'll get used to it eventually... I think your driver's taken a wrong turn.'

The route to the Palvetti headquarters had become as familiar to her as her old route to the White's Events building had been.

'We're not going to the office.'

'Where are we going, then?'

His smile was knowing. 'You'll see.'

Minutes later they arrived at what was unmistakably a heliport. The gleaming black helicopter was the giveaway.

'Have you ever been in a helicopter?'

'I've never even seen one that's not in the air. Is this yours?'

He grinned.

Her awe increased when they climbed inside the luxurious cabin and she found six seats in rows of three set opposite each other and covered in the softest cream leather upholstery.

She strapped herself in beside Alessio and moments later felt the slightest dip in her stomach as the pilot lifted the craft from the ground.

'Where are you taking me?' she asked.

'To where the magic happens,' he answered enigmatically.

Time flew as quickly as the helicopter. Beth gazed out of the window and watched as they left the urban sprawl of Milan behind. Soon, she saw mountains in the distance and, as they flew closer, expanses of water gleaming under the morning sun.

Her heart leapt. 'Is that Lake Como?'

'Excellent deduction.'

The beauty of what lay beneath took her breath away and she forgot all about their destination until she realised they were losing altitude. At the foot of two mountains lay a sprawling mediaeval building with sand-coloured walls and red roof tiles built as a square ring around a vast courtyard.

They landed a short distance from it and, when they climbed out, she noticed the landing site was part of the complex, the entire perimeter surrounded by thick trees. She counted eight security guards patrolling the area.

She looked at Alessio.

His lips curved. 'You wanted to see the workshop…here we are.'

'*This* is the workshop?'

She'd imagined an ordinary industrial building in an ordinary industrial setting, not something that looked as if it had been an important monastery in a previous life set in the most glorious landscape imaginable.

They were driven through the vast grounds on a golf buggy, past a manned checkpoint and through the alarmed gates into the compound itself.

Alessio enjoyed watching Beth's stunned reaction to it all.

His fellow directors could go to hell, he thought coldly.

He'd called them into the boardroom on his return from the workshop and torn a strip off them for making his wife feel unwanted and disliked.

'You cannot expect us to accept her like this,' Carla had shouted back at him. 'When is she going to start taking the business seriously?'

'She *is* taking it seriously'

'Then where is she? Why is she not here?'

'She's gone home.'

'Home?' Carla had scorned. 'While the rest of us are here working? We are coming into our busiest time with the Christmas period about to start and she's at home with her feet up?'

Before Alessio could defend his wife, Gina had cut in to back up her sister. 'She's not like us. She's not business-minded. All week she has shadowed me and it is obvious she wants to be somewhere else.'

'Is that surprising when you make no effort to put her at ease?'

'She's spent the week looking at her watch!

We try to forget she was Domenico's friend but she doesn't make it easy. She should try to fit in with us.'

At that, Alessio had slammed his fist on the table. 'She is doing her best! If I find that *any* of you treat her with anything less than respect from this point on, I will clear your offices personally.'

He drove thoughts of his family aside when they stepped into the spacious reception room. He introduced Beth to the smiling receptionist, used his thumbprint to sign himself in then set Beth up with her own thumbprint.

If his family didn't like it, then tough.

'Is this entire building the workshop?' she asked.

'Only the east wing. The other wings are for our laboratories.'

'I thought they were in separate locations.'

'Not in a decade. We had a major renovation programme and brought it all under one roof.'

'Why here?' Her eyes were alight with curiosity.

'This is where the Palvettis are from.'

'Lake Como? I thought you were from Milan.'

'Not originally. My great-grandfather had a

small workshop on the ground floor of the family home in a town a kilometre from here. He was taught the craft by his own father—jewellery making was the family trade for generations before Palvetti as we know it today came into being.'

He pushed open the double doors to the right and they entered the art studio. Beth's attention was captured by the intricate designs being worked on and she studied them while Alessio recounted his family history.

'After the war, when Europe and the world itself was recovering from all the terrible things that had occurred during it, a Venetian got lost on his way back to his holiday villa by the lake. He knocked on the workshop door for directions and fell in love with a ring my great-grandfather was making. He commissioned a ring for his wife. She showed it to her friends. Those who could afford it ordered bespoke creations too. Word spread. There were not enough hours in the day for him to take all the commissions, which pushed the prices up, which in itself added to the allure. My great-grandmother recognised this—where my great-grandfather had the talent, she had the business brain.'

'Rare that she was allowed to use it in those days,' Beth commented.

'It was. I never met her but my father described her as a formidable lady. She recognised that our unique selling point was exclusivity and mystique. She was the driving force behind the Palvetti we are today. No interviews and, at the time, no advertising or marketing. To wear our jewellery and our scents—those were her idea too—you had to be in the club to know about it and you had to be wealthy to be able to afford it. My grandfather and his siblings all joined the company when they turned eighteen and it's been Palvetti owned and controlled ever since.'

'What happened to the house where it all began?'

'One of my cousins owns it.'

The art studio done with, they went through to the next room—the workshop itself.

Beth gaped at the scale of it and wondered if Alessio's great-grandparents had ever envisaged their creations being made in a place like this.

Work benches and tools of all shapes and sizes lay as far as the eye could see, instruments Beth didn't recognise, a scent in the air she didn't recognise either, but which contained a metallic tang, a chaotic yet somehow orderly mess.

A dozen people in protective overcoats worked at their benches, too engrossed in the intricacy of their creations to pay attention to them other than one tall, skinny man who hurried over to greet them.

Alessio introduced him as his cousin, Gianluigi.

Gianluigi, it quickly transpired, ran the workshop. He was also Carla's and Gina's brother, a fact made more shocking by him greeting Beth with real warmth and enthusiastically showing what he was working on: a thick gold bangle half-encrusted with gleaming jewels of differing colours. He explained it was part of a set commissioned by a sheikh for his new bride.

Beth couldn't resist asking the price.

'The whole set is six million euros.'

A month ago, the price would have made her eyes pop out.

'It's beautiful,' she said with feeling. 'I am in awe of your talent.'

When they left the workshop and were back

in the reception room, she said to Alessio, 'I didn't realise a Palvetti still made the jewellery.'

'Gianluigi's not the only one. His eldest daughter wants to take an apprenticeship in the workshop when she finishes school. Four of our jewellery makers and goldsmiths are family members. There are six of us working in the laboratories too. I told you—there is a role in our company to suit everyone.'

He opened the door on the other side of the reception room and suddenly Beth found herself transported into a futuristic world of science fiction fantasy, all clean white lines and people in white overcoats.

The deeper they explored, the more there was to see: the indoor greenhouse, the room with dried harvested ingredients, a distillery...even a packaging room. Everything there to create the wonderful scents which pervaded the air with every step she took from conception to finished product. There was so much to it, so many rooms to explore and people with differing roles to talk to, that she could hardly take it all in.

Their tour ended two hours after it started in a vast meeting room, the only space in the building to have retained its mediaeval roots. She could imagine dozens of monks dining together in this room amidst the exposed ancient stone walls and oak flooring.

Refreshments were brought in to them. Beth stood at a lead-paned window, soaking in the glorious views and nibbling on a pastry, her mind racing.

Alessio watched her closely just as he'd watched her closely throughout the tour. He'd never seen her so animated or her eyes shine so brightly. They shone now as she turned from the window to face him.

'You should hold a party here.'

He raised a brow at this outrageous suggestion but a dreamy expression had come over Beth's face and she didn't notice.

'A party for your richest clients. An exclusive party...'

His ears suddenly pricked up. 'Go on.'

She closed her eyes and swayed. 'You invite a select few. Ten at the most. And partners. We tell them to meet in Milan and then helicopter them in blindfolded...no, blindfolds are taking secrecy too far. They tour specially selected parts of the laboratories and are allowed to smell the scents in production. You give them demonstrations of various processes…but keep them away from the workshop; there's no glamour there, and it's good to retain some mystique. Once their experience in the laboratory is over, they're brought into this meeting room which is transformed into a wonderland. The finest Palvetti jewellery will be discreetly displayed and admired. The guests are greeted by a string quartet playing beautiful music, real-life models sprayed in gold standing in artful positions to become human statues, delicious canapés, champagne…

'When the guests leave, it's with a gift-wrapped box containing their own specially produced scent and a specially crafted bracelet for the ladies and cufflinks for the gentlemen.'

For a moment he was so taken with watching her speak, the dreaminess on the beautiful face, the rise and fall of her breasts beneath her pale green shirt-dress, that the words she'd actually said took a little longer than they should have to land in his brain.

His throat was dry as he spoke. 'What would be the purpose?'

Her eyes snapped open. 'To make them feel

special. You said your great-grandmother thought of Palvetti as being like a club that you had to be in the know about to be a part of. A party would be an extension of that. The more exclusive and secret it is, the more the guests won't be able to resist boasting to their rich friends about it. Those friends will be green with envy and spend even more money on bespoke jewellery in the hope of one day getting their own special invitation...'

She suddenly stopped talking, gave an embarrassed laugh and reached for her coffee. 'Sorry, my imagination ran away with me there.'

He shook his head slowly, his mind bringing to life Beth's vision that had sprung from nowhere. 'That is an incredible idea.'

She was incredible. Beautiful, sexy and burning with ideas that just needed a conduit into which to unleash them.

'It is?'

'A secret, exclusive party that they won't be able to resist talking about. If we host it in a month, there will be time for word to reach the ears of those who would want to place orders in time for Christmas.'

'A month doesn't give you much time.' She

flicked a crumb of pastry off the skirt of her dress.

'You organised a masquerade ball in six weeks. If anyone can pull this off, you can.'

Her gaze shot up to meet his. *'Me?'*

'Who better?' he asked nonchalantly. 'This is the perfect role for you.'

'But I'm shadowing Marcello next week and—'

'Not any more.' His wife's shadowing days were over. Gina was right. Beth wasn't business-minded, not in the way needed to run a Palvetti department. She was creative. She thrived on projects. Chaining her to an office desk would suck the life out of her.

She chewed her lips with an expression on her face that concerned him.

'Don't you want to do it?'

'I do...' She raised her shoulders and grimaced. 'I'm just thinking. Four weeks is no time at all. It'll mean I have to work weekends.'

'You object to weekends?' He hadn't got her to work any yet, mostly because he'd been easing her into the business slowly so as not to overwhelm her any more than she already was.

'I see little enough of Dom as it is without losing my weekends with him.'

Alessio dragged his fingers through his hair, knowing exactly what his cousins would say if they heard Beth speaking like this.

He also knew what they would say if they heard his response. They would be outraged. 'We will provide you with enough staff that working weekends will be unnecessary.'

The light that shone from her face at his words was bright enough for him to feel as if he'd been injected with sunrays.

To hell with his cousins.

He would let Beth arrange the party and, once it was done, create a permanent role for her within the company as bespoke as any of the jewellery they created.

His mind made up, the weight he'd carried on his shoulders since Beth's confession that she was overwhelmed at work and felt hated by his family lifted.

If Beth had been told three weeks ago that she would be dining in a two-Michelin-starred restaurant in Milan that had the appearance of an art gallery with Alessio Palvetti as her husband, their fellow diners a Chinese business-man and his translator, she would have thought the person doing the telling was a crank. The very notion would have been so preposterous that she'd have advised them to see a doctor.

But here she was.

The food, as to be expected, was divine: an eleven-course tasting menu, each course served with its own specially selected accompanying wine.

Her taste-buds thought they'd died and gone to heaven, especially when she ate the scallops served with fennel, coral mayonnaise, capers and raspberry vinegar, ingredients she would never have thought should be put together. She resisted the urge to steal the tiny portion left on the translator's plate.

Her husband sat beside her. He ate with gusto too, although she noticed he drank half the amount of wine as the businessman. Between courses he hooked an arm casually around the back of her chair. She liked the casual posses-siveness of the gesture. She hated that she liked it, not out of any feminist ideals, but because she knew the danger.

Their trip to the workshop had changed everything.

She practically buzzed with excitement... She could hardly believe he'd listened to her rambling thoughts and not only thought them a good idea but wanted her to go ahead and do it! Finally, a project she could get her teeth into, doing something she was good at and which she enjoyed.

Finally, she understood what Alessio meant about there being a role for everyone in Palvetti. It gave her hope for Dom too. When he grew up he would find a place in the family business into which to carve his own niche.

Even if professional pride would not allow her to do anything but her best at this, for Alessio she would go even further. For Alessio she would do everything she could to make this party perfect and justify his faith in her.

That faith blew her mind.

It meant so much.

Her feelings for him were becoming harder to contain. For an ordinary married couple this would be a good thing, but there was nothing ordinary about their marriage, and she continually had to remind herself of that.

Trying her hardest to push her thoughts aside, she concentrated on the conversation at hand.

Their trip to Lake Como had given her a greater understanding of the business and let her see with her own eyes Alessio's fierce pride in both the business and his family. He was doing his best to find her a role within it and she was determined to play her part too and be the best asset she could be.

Eventually, the meal was over and the businessman messaged his driver to collect him while Alessio picked up the tab.

When they were seated in the back of their car, Alessio turned to her. 'Ready for something different?'

'What do you mean?'

'That the night is young.' His lips quirked. 'I'd hate for you to think my idea of a good night out is a boring business dinner.'

She tried not to get excited. 'You're taking me out?'

'Do you want to? Dom will be asleep so we don't need to rush back for him.'

'Are we going to do something fun?'

'That's the idea.' His lips quirked again. 'I got the distinct impression that you were disappointed when I told you tonight's meal was a business dinner.'

Beth beamed. Her husband's perceptiveness was a constant source of astonishment.

He pressed the intercom button and spoke to his driver. 'Take us to Club Giroud.'

A few minutes later and they were driving through the district in which she'd spent an extortionate amount of Alessio's money, shortly coming to a stop in a vibrant area packed with people dressed to the nines enjoying the best of Milan's nightlife.

Excitement filled her. Beth hadn't been on a night out since before Dom's birth.

Laughter filled her ears when she stepped out of the car and new aromas wafted into her nose, different scents from the day. In the near distance she spotted the Duomo twinkling under the moonlit sky.

She didn't get the chance to take much more in for Alessio opened a nondescript door and they entered a nondescript room where two burly men stood guarding a second door. On the wall beside it was a square box. Alessio pressed a button and it flashed green. Then he put his face to it.

A moment later the men stepped aside and the door they'd been guarding opened.

How many gasps of awe could a woman make in a lifetime? Beth wondered. There was nothing nondescript about this reception room, where Alessio went to the highly polished desk and signed them in, and nothing nondescript about the warren of rooms they passed in this luxurious club that had an eclectic, buzzing atmosphere.

There was nothing nondescript about the clientele either. On their walk through it she saw more diamonds than in a Palvetti jewellery store and she spotted more than a few famous faces.

On the third floor he led them to a room where the decibel level was lower than in many they'd passed to reach it.

A hostess greeted them and led them to a corner table with two single armchairs facing each other separated by a glass table. Alessio had removed his tie in the car and now placed his jacket on the back of his armchair.

'What is this place?' Beth asked once they'd ordered their drinks and were alone.

'A private members' club. There are rooms

for all occasions and requirements. I thought we could have a drink in here to start and then you can choose what you want to do. We can play cards in the casino room…whatever you want.'

She took her Rossini cocktail from the returning hostess with a murmured thanks and had a long drink of it. 'I want to dance.'

Alessio took a long drink of his too. 'What do you like to dance to?'

'Stuff with a funky beat. Funnily enough, that's not the kind of music I like to listen to.'

'Which is?'

'Edgier music. Rock. What about you?'

'My life doesn't leave much time for music.'

'There's always time. I always used to have music playing when I worked.' If ever she got her own office she would get a radio and play music to her heart's content.

'I find it a distraction. There's plenty of time for music when I retire.'

'But that's decades away.'

'And I will have decades left to enjoy my life and all the world's music.'

'You don't know that. Life's fragile. No one knows what's around the corner.' She thought of her parents. She thought of Caroline and Domenico. 'Look at your brother: gone before he could fulfil his dreams.'

His expression darkened almost imperceptibly.

'I know you're dismissive of his music but he *was* talented.'

The strong nostrils flared.

Reading between the lines of what Domenico had told her of their relationship, and Alessio's own version of events, their estrangement had been a long time in the making. Domenico had blinded himself to Alessio's qualities and Alessio had done the same.

It was time her husband learned his brother had had good qualities.

Ignoring the growing darkness of his stare, she said, 'He formed a band in London. That's how Caroline and I met him—they were playing a gig in a venue near our flat. They were brilliant and Domenico was the creative force behind it. They had a real following behind them and were in talks about a record deal when he had the accident. I wonder...'

She sighed and grazed her teeth over her lips. 'Wonder what?'

'I wonder if the pressure of being a Palvetti and living under your shadow stifled him when he was living here. Your parents went out of their way to support him but, being here, I can see the pressure he must have been under. Domenico was a sensitive soul who felt things deeply. He wasn't designed for the corporate world.'

There was intensity in the emerald stare on her but no anger.

'The Domenico I knew was happy,' she told him softly. 'He never had much money but he had Caroline, friends, his band, a life. When Caroline fell pregnant they were the happiest souls on earth. I was so envious of the love they found together. They were soul mates. I longed for that…' She shook her head away from thoughts that could never be. 'Her diagnosis devastated him.'

He shifted in his seat. 'It was cancer, wasn't it?'

She nodded. 'It was the same hereditary strain that killed her mother, grandmother and an aunt too.'

Alessio thought hard, swirling his glass of

Scotch absently. 'She had the diagnosis before Dom was born?'

It was not something he had thought about before, even though he'd known she'd died when Dom was only three months old.

'Caroline was five months' pregnant when she found the lump in her breast. She refused to have any treatment because she knew it would harm the baby.'

He swore, his chest tightening so hard he could hardly breathe. 'Would treatment have saved her?'

'We don't know. Possibly. But she wouldn't have taken it even if they'd guaranteed her survival, not if there was the slightest chance of it harming Dom.'

'She knew refusing the treatment would kill her?'

'Yes. And your brother did too.'

His head spun as if all the alcohol he'd consumed that evening had hit him at once.

And as he thought of excess alcohol he remembered the coroner's report into his brother's death and his initial surprise at the findings. His brother had been born a selfish bastard but he'd never been much of a drinker.

He put the dates together. Caroline was diagnosed with cancer at five months' pregnant. A month later, Domenico was the one lying dead.

'He begged her to have the treatment but her mind was made up,' Beth whispered into the silence. 'He started drinking heavily because he couldn't cope. Caroline was his life. The only time he was truly sober in the weeks before his death was when they got the wills drawn up.'

A stab of anger cut through him at this unwitting confirmation of his brother's selfishness. Domenico's pregnant wife had received a terminal diagnosis and all he'd been able to do was hit the bottle?

He downed what was left of his Scotch but his throat had become so constricted it was an effort to swallow it.

Alessio and Domenico had always been different. They'd been brothers but they'd not had much in the way of a brotherly relationship.

The truth was, they had despised each other.

Seeing tears swim in Beth's eyes only made him feel more wretched.

'I brought you here to enjoy yourself, not to make you cry.'

'You haven't.' She contorted her face into a smile. 'It's still raw. Caroline.'

'I get that.'

Her eyes held his. 'Do you miss him at all?'

'Domenico?'

She nodded.

'No.' It was an admission that weighed on his conscience. 'I miss my mother, but I think to miss someone you have to know them, and I never knew my brother.'

Once Alessio had gone to boarding school, any brotherly bond had been severed. He'd been too disdainful of his brother's life choices to get to know him as an adult.

Placing his empty glass on the table, he got to his feet and held out a hand. 'I promised you a dance.'

This time her smile was a notch brighter.

She slipped her much smaller hand into his and held it tightly as he guided her to the dance room, already packed with people letting their hair down to the thudding beats.

When he pulled Beth into his arms and they found a rhythm together that came as naturally as breathing, all he could think was that he'd forced her into a life she'd never wanted and from which she could never escape. She would never have the chance to build true happiness for herself as Domenico had done before his death.

She would never find the love she'd longed for.

Alessio had taken that from her.

CHAPTER ELEVEN

'YOU HAVE AGREED to *what*?'

Alessio folded his arms across his chest and merely stared at Gina. He would not repeat himself.

He had called the directors into the boardroom to share the innovative idea his wife had come up with, not to be on the receiving end of yet more attitude. He was rapidly losing patience with the cousin to whom he had always been closest.

Gina put her hands on the table and spoke through gritted teeth. 'A party in our production facility? You are out of your mind.'

Carla and Marcello, however, both had thoughtful expressions on their faces. Neither had said anything since Alessio had explained Beth's idea.

'Our production facility is located in one of the most beautiful places on God's earth in a converted monastery,' he reminded them icily.

'The external architecture rivals any of the lakeside villas for beauty.'

'I do not deny that. My point is that our most sacred secrets are kept within its walls and you want to open it up to the public.'

'No, we want to host an intimate party for no more than ten of our most lucrative clients.'

'And their partners. And bespoke gifts when they leave? How much is it going to cost?'

'A lot,' he admitted, unperturbed. The more he'd thought about it over the weekend, the more genius he'd come to think the idea. 'Whatever we spend will be recouped. If this is played well it could be more lucrative than the necklace that actress wore at the Hollywood awards ceremony.' Palvetti refused to lend their jewellery for award ceremonies but this particular actress had a doting husband who happened to be a filthy-rich movie producer. A stroke of luck had seen her win the best actress role. She had been on the front cover of every major newspaper across the world, wearing her Palvetti necklace.

'*If,*' she seethed. 'That has big implications for such a small word.'

'Beth can pull it off. I've seen her work and

this project will allow you to see how hard she works when it's something she's passionate about. You will see what a great asset she can be for us.'

Gina stared at him then burst into a peal of laughter. 'That's what this is about? You are opening up our facility to please your little pet? You would give away our secrets just to make her happy?'

Before he'd even registered his backside leaving his chair, Alessio was on his feet, his fists clenched.

'Do you forget who you are talking to?' he asked, chest heaving, controlling his voice by a thread.

If Gina had been a man he would have thrown himself across the boardroom table and pinned her to the floor.

How dared she call Beth a pet when *she* was the one who'd made his wife feel like an unwanted stray?

'Do you forget who *you* are talking to?' But, for all the bravado of Gina's tone, her face had turned white. 'The business is not yours alone, Alessio. I was voted onto the board of directors for the same reasons you were. My voice is as valid as yours.'

'Not when your voice speaks only poison.'

'Someone has to say it. I have agreed with your insistence that I be respectful to her, and I will abide by it, but I will not be party to an event that could be the ruin of us.'

Breathing deeply to control the fury racketing through him, he turned his attention to Carla and Marcello. Both kept their eyes fixed on the table. 'We will take a vote. Normal rules apply. But if you all agree that hosting an exclusive party for our most select guests is the potential ruin of us then I stand down from the board and the business.'

That made them look up.

'I mean it. I will not stay if you doubt my judgement or my motives. One of you can take control.' He had earned enough from his time at Palvetti in the form of salary and bonuses to need never work again ten lifetimes over. 'All those in favour of the party, raise your hands.'

He held his hand up then held his breath.

Carla lifted her eyes and looked at him. Then she slowly raised her hand.

Gina glared at her sister.

He had won. In the event of a tie, Alessio had the casting vote.

But then Marcello looked up from his spot on the table and looked straight at his furious wife. 'I'm sorry, Gina. I trust Alessio and I think this could work.'

Then he too raised his hand.

The slam of the boardroom door as Gina stormed out reverberated through the floor.

Beth was engrossed with writing her initial plans with old-fashioned pen and paper when she heard Alessio enter his office and close the door behind him.

'How did it go?' she asked, not looking up.

This was the first time she'd gone to the office in a week without the chimes of doom playing in her head, and she'd got stuck straight into writing down all the thoughts for the party that had percolated in her head over the weekend while Alessio filled in the other directors in about it.

She wrote 'scented truffles' down and underlined it. Was there such a thing? Could they lace confectionery with perfume without killing anyone?

'Alessio?' She looked up from her work, wondering why he hadn't responded, and found him propped against the adjoining door of their offices.

There had been no discussion about it but to Beth's mind this was her permanent office now. The first thing she'd done when arriving at headquarters that morning was to take all her stuff out of the box room Gina had made her work from and move it back in here.

She liked *this* office. She liked being close to Alessio. She liked that she could look up from her desk whenever she wanted and see the man she…

Her eyes met his.

There was something in his stare, a starkness that made her heart expand to fill her chest.

She gazed into those emerald eyes with emotions surging through her, crashing through her blood and pounding in her head, diving to deepen the breaths straining to escape from her lungs.

Suddenly her heart could expand no more. It exploded. Shockwaves followed its wake, rippling in her veins like a thousand tsunamis.

Alessio couldn't tear his eyes from Beth's. His feet felt weighted to the floor.

From his position at the doorway, he'd observed her with a compression in his chest, head bowed in concentration, silky dark hair spilling around her shoulders and onto her desk.

Where had the white-hot rage that had consumed him minutes ago come from? When he would have turned his back on everything for her, his business and his family?

He would have walked away from everything he'd spent his life working for. For her.

When she'd lifted her head and those chocolate eyes had met his, the compression had reached a peak. Something shifted inside him and a pain like nothing he had experienced before ripped through him.

He felt as if he'd been shot.

The silence in the office was absolute. Other than his heart. It thumped harder and stronger in his chest than he had ever felt it do before.

If he strained his ears he was certain he'd be able to hear Beth's heart beating too.

Their eyes stayed locked together.

Moving of its own accord, his hand reached behind him to pull the door shut.

He put one foot in front of the other.

He inhaled her scent before he reached her. It dove into him.

And then he stood before her and stared at her beautiful face. But Beth's beauty ran deeper than merely skin-deep. She had beauty in her core and that beauty was shining at him.

Her face tilted up to his. Her breaths were as heavy as his own but it was the hunger staring back at him... It pulsed in the swirl of her eyes, lived in the colour rising high on her cheeks.

He didn't know who made the first move but one moment they were gazing wordlessly at each other, the next they were pressed tightly together, her arms hooked around his neck, his arms tight around her waist, mouths fused, tongues dancing, her sweet taste filling him.

And *how* it filled him.

Suddenly he was consumed with the need to possess her and devour her whole.

Within seconds he'd lifted her so she was sat on her desk, the skirt of her dress bunched around her waist.

Her fingers dug into the base of his skull before she dragged her hands over his shoulders and placed her palms on his beating chest.

He broke the kiss and stared into her eyes but found only the same madness that had taken him in its grip.

With a loud groan he kissed her again, hard, hungry, a starving man desperate for the sustenance only she could provide.

In a tangle of fingers and kisses razed over cheeks and necks they worked together to free his arousal from the confines of his trousers, and then he was pulling down her knickers, which she kicked free with her feet, and then he was standing between her parted thighs and with one thrust buried deep inside her tight, sodden heat.

Their lips fused together and he pounded into her with an urgency heightened beyond anything he'd ever known before. And she matched him. He held her tightly around her back while her hands cradled his head, nails scraping against his scalp. Their gasps were drowned in each other's mouths.

Somehow, he was able to hold his release until she wrenched her mouth from his and pressed her lips tightly into his neck. He felt a thickening drag him deeper and deeper inside her and he lost himself in a climax so powerful, the walls around him faded to a blurry nothing.

It felt as if for ever had passed before he returned to the here and now and when he arrived…

Sanity returned in a single beat.

He blinked then stared into Beth's dazed eyes.

Sanity must have returned to her too for they broke apart at the same time.

Not a single word was spoken as they hurriedly straightened their clothing and smoothed their hair.

He welcomed the brief distraction.

Never in his life had he lost control like that.

Madness had taken him in its clutches.

Beth found it best to concentrate on keeping herself upright on legs that felt as if spaghetti had replaced the bones rather than dissect what had just exploded between them.

Alessio had never laid a finger on her outside the bedroom before. Not even a kiss to her cheek. There had been nothing, and now this…?

A loud knock on his office door almost had her jumping out of her skin.

Her eyes darted to his.

He held her gaze for a long moment before giving a tight smile. His throat moved before he said, 'Work calls.'

His long legs carried him out of her office and into his own. She was grateful he closed the adjoining door behind him. It gave her the privacy she needed to sink onto her chair and attempt to control the ragged beats of her heart.

After dragging in enough lungsful of air to give oxygen to her dazed brain, she tried to think with a bit more coherence.

But her thoughts were all wrapped up in her husband and the wild emotions for him still racing through her entire being.

Alessio was a much better man than she could have dreamed. He could be ruthless. If he wanted something he would stop at nothing until he had it. But he could also be tender. He could be thoughtful. He listened.

He'd effectively blackmailed her into this life but her happiness mattered to him.

It had been a long time since her happiness had mattered to anyone.

The week that followed was busy for Beth. Not only did she have the party at the production facility to organise but it was Dom's first birthday that weekend and she was arranging a party to celebrate that.

To think only two months ago she'd worried about affording even the most basic of presents for him and had fretted that he would be missing out with only herself there to blow out the candles of his cake. Alessio had assured her those of his cousins with small children would attend and that Dom would finally meet the children he would grow up with and one day run Palvetti with.

As she also had the other party to work on, Alessio had now moved her to another, larger office and given her the promised staff to assist her. It meant she no longer worked in the adjoining office to his which, she told herself, was a good thing.

The encounter, for want of a better word, between them on her desk on Monday...

She couldn't rid herself of the images from it.

There had been no chance of a repeat. If anything, Alessio had gone to even greater lengths to keep a physical distance at work. He never came within arm's reach of her, never intimated by word or deed that he thought of her intimately at all. Were it not for the fire they stoked beneath the sheets every night, she could easily believe he had no sexual feelings for her at all.

She wished she had his discipline. She supposed it was because sex and all the feelings that went with it were still so new to her, but she'd become utterly consumed by him. It was like a sickness had infected her.

When he walked into her office late Friday afternoon, she had to strain with all her might not to smile too widely.

'How are you getting on?' he asked.

'Great!' She might have to hide her enthusiasm at her husband's presence in her office but she didn't have to hide her enthusiasm for the party she was planning. 'The guests you selected have all got back to me and are all able to attend. What do you think about these for the canapés?' She clicked her computer for him to see the list.

He stood behind her to peer over her shoulder.

Beth crossed her legs in a futile attempt to nullify the heat that seeped through her and leaned forward so she didn't give in to the temptation to lean her head back against his chest.

'Citrus-cured sea bass on blinis with Ossetra caviar and crème fraiche,' he read aloud, his breath hot in her hair. 'Sounds good.'

She swallowed as the citrusy undertone of his cologne swirled into her senses. 'The caterers will send samples of all the canapés so we can try them first and make any changes needed.'

A long, muscular arm reached over her desk, long fingers wrapping over her hand to take control of the mouse and scroll through the other canapé choices.

Her throat ran dry.

Then she realised the hand holding hers to control the mouse had stopped scrolling. She could no longer hear his breaths...

She turned her face and found emerald eyes fixed on her.

Then the dark lashes swept before her as his mouth closed in on...

'I should have known I'd find you here.'

They jumped apart. Gina's entrance to Beth's office was as unexpected and as volatile as a grenade.

Not even casting a glance at Beth, she immediately addressed Alessio, who strode over to her, gabbling away in Italian at high speed.

Beth didn't have the faintest idea what they were talking about and watched, torn between bemusement and outrage, as they conversed.

She knew perfectly well Gina was doing this deliberately. Shutting Beth out. She'd hardly acknowledged Beth all week.

After a minute of this high-speed chat, Gina put her hands on Alessio's shoulders and kissed his cheeks. '*Ciao*, Alessio.'

'*Ciao*, Gina.'

But when she reached the door she turned back to him and said in perfect English, 'Did you get the information I sent to you about Quilton House?'

Alarm bells immediately clanged loudly in Beth's head. She knew that name.

He nodded.

'Places are taken very quickly. You need to get his name down now.'

As Gina sashayed out of his office, Alessio was aware of Beth, risen to her feet, staring at him, her face flushed.

'Quilton House?' she said slowly. 'As in the boarding school?'

'Yes. It's where all Palvetti children go.'

'You want to send Dom there?'

'It's one of the best schools in the world,' Alessio told her calmly, although there was little in the way of calmness inside him.

If Gina hadn't chosen that moment to barge into Beth's office he would have kissed her.

As he knew all too well, one kiss from Beth was never enough. Her kisses were like a drug to him. One press of her lips to his and one taste of her sweet breath and he wanted more. He craved more.

'The education there is second to none.'

'I don't want him to go to boarding school.'

'All Palvetti children go to boarding school. It teaches them resilience and independence.'

'He can learn that at a school in Milan. He's hardly been here a month and you want to send him away?'

'He won't go for years, *bella*. I promise you, he will *thrive* there.'

'I don't care if he doesn't have to go until he's twenty-one, I don't want him to go full-stop.'

'I'm afraid the issue is not up for debate. Dom is a Palvetti and he will go to boarding school, as all our children do. You have ten years to get used to the idea.'

Alessio had no wish to be hard about it but Beth needed to learn resilience as much as Dom did. He'd made many allowances for the bond they shared, such as not requiring her to work weekends so she and Dom could spend time together, but he would have to start weaning them apart sooner rather than later otherwise the separation, when it came, would hit them both too hard.

Her face had drained of colour. She gazed at him with a loathing he hadn't seen since he'd told her about the pre-nuptial agreement.

And then she moved, sweeping her arm across her desk to send the files and other bits and pieces she had on it flying in all directions.

'I will never get used to the idea!' She seethed. 'This is *exactly* why your brother and Caroline made me his guardian. Domenico knew if you got your hands on him you would send him away, and he was right.'

'It's not a case of sending him away. It's a matter of providing him with a world-class education at a school that will mould him into a fully rounded—'

'That's *our* job,' she cried. 'That's what being a parent's all about. A school won't love him or nurture him. Your brother *hated* that boarding school. He always said it was the worst experience of his life.'

'Yes, he hated Quilton House, which is why our parents transferred him to a different school of his choosing after only one year, one that had a different ethos and embraced the arts and creativity.'

There was a flicker of confusion on the angry face.

'Did he forget to tell you that part?' he asked scathingly. 'Have you not yet realised my brother was prone to exaggeration? He was always selective in his truths.'

'It doesn't change that he hated boarding school.'

'*One* child out of dozens of us hated it. Ask any of the rest of us—we all, every one of us, thrived there.'

'Considering your family are a bunch of cold fish, that doesn't fill me with any confidence.'

He gritted his teeth lest he started shouting too. To have his family described in such a way was a personal slight on him too. 'It is an excellent school with excellent pastoral care. I accept Domenico was different to the rest of us, almost a hippy in his outlook, but that doesn't mean his son will be. With my guidance—'

'*Your* guidance?' She had a look on her face that made Alessio glad she had nothing left on her desk. He was quite sure she would have thrown it at him.

'Yes, *bella*. *My* guidance.' Her scorn had him clinging to his temper by a whisker. 'By the time Dom graduates from university, he will have all the tools he needs to take his place here in a role that suits and fulfils him. I'm sorry if this displeases you, but it is for his benefit, and not up for debate… Where are you going?'

Beth had grabbed her bag and stormed to the door.

'I'm going home,' she spat. 'Sorry if it *displeases* you but, seeing as you're planning to send my son away, I'm going to spend as much time with him as I can while I can.'

'Beth…'

'And this discussion isn't over. Not by a long chalk.'

Beth slammed the door shut behind her and practically ran down the corridor. Too impatient to get out of this place and get home to Dom to wait for the lift, she hurled herself down the stairs.

The *hateful* man.

And how stupid was she?

The weeks spent sharing his bed and working by his side had made her forget that, at heart, her husband was a Palvetti to his core and had all the power in their marriage.

If he wanted to send Dom to boarding school, she had no idea how she was supposed to stop him. Super-glue herself to Dom the day he turned eleven?

Alessio would probably get around that obstacle by sending her with him.

CHAPTER TWELVE

BETH DIDN'T FEEL much calmer when Alessio returned home but the extra time she'd spent with Dom had soothed her fractious nerves a little.

But only a little.

All this talk of boarding school had reinforced how desperately she missed being with him.

If Dom wasn't such an early riser she would only see him at weekends. The other senior Palvettis all worked weekends. They never switched off.

She understood why. They worked hard to secure the business for the next generation but it was too much. For Beth, it was too much.

There was no way she could cope with Dom being sent to boarding school.

If it came to it, she would move to England to be close to him, she vowed. If Alessio didn't like it, then…

She blinked back tears. She didn't want Dom, now snuggled on her lap, guzzling his evening bottle, to see her cry.

This was what she'd signed up for. She'd married Alessio knowing who he was and what he stood for. It was her own fault that she'd allowed her head to be turned by the joy she found in his love-making, and the great concessions he'd made to help her fit into his world and find fulfilment in it, and forgotten who he was at heart.

She hated that this extra time with Dom was spent thinking about Alessio.

And she hated that, when her husband put his head around the nursery door, her heart thumped.

Dom, however, was thrilled to see him, pushed the bottle from his mouth and held his arms out for a cuddle.

She noted the surprise on Alessio's face and tried hard to hold on to her loathing when he strode over and took Dom from her.

He lifted the squealing child into the air and carried him around the room.

Dom's delight at this...

How could Alessio even contemplate sending him away? Where did he keep his heart? Locked in a cage?

Soon, Alessio kissed Dom's cheek and handed him back to Beth.

Dom immediately grabbed the half-drunk bottle from her hand and shoved it in his mouth.

'Clever boy,' Alessio said in delight, then looked at Beth. 'Dinner will be ready in ten minutes.'

She gave a brittle smile. 'I ate with Dom earlier.'

He contemplated her silently, nodded and left the room.

'How long's this silent treatment going to last?' Alessio had eaten his dinner alone then come to his bedroom to find Beth in bed, turned on her side, reading a book. She hadn't acknowledged him when he'd entered, hadn't answered when he'd said he was taking a shower or turned to look at him when he'd climbed into the bed beside her and found her wearing a pair of pyjamas.

After all this, it didn't surprise him that she didn't answer.

His own anger at their argument had cooled considerably.

He'd thought long and hard about it in the intervening hours with increasing discomfort. Arguments and differences of opinion were a fact of life but this was now the second time he'd lost his temper in the office. Twice in one week after fifteen years of always keeping a cool head and seeing things from a logical standpoint. When those around him shouted to make their voices heard, he sat back and waited for calm.

What was it about Beth that could slide under his skin so effectively?

He'd been seconds from making love to her in the office again too.

'Beth...' He thought of the best words to use to bring about peace between them. He would not apologise for wanting the best for his nephew. He settled on, 'I'm sorry you're upset.'

She rolled onto her back and placed the book face-down on her stomach. She inhaled sharply and fixed her gaze to the ceiling. 'I'm not upset, Alessio. I'm angry. I don't care if it's tradi-tional for your family to dump all your children at boarding school, I will never accept Dom going. It's cruel and barbaric.'

He bit back a curse. The time she'd had to think had not softened her stance in the slightest. 'I told you, the school takes its pastoral care seriously.'

'Does that stop children feeling homesick?' she challenged.

'I never suffered homesickness.'

'Never? Not even once?'

'I loved my time there.' And he had. The days had been long but full: lessons, clubs, sports; plenty for a growing adolescent to get his teeth into. He'd made some great friends, shared some great experiences...what was there not to like?

But those were not the things that would give Beth the assurance she needed right then.

'If I ever suffered a low moment—which I don't remember suffering from—there was always the thought of my grandparents coming to visit on the scheduled family weekends to keep me going.'

'Your grandparents? Not your parents?'

'My parents were too busy working.'

'Too busy to visit their kids at their boarding school in a foreign country when every Palvetti has their own private jet? You think that's normal?'

He sighed in exasperation. 'It is for us. It doesn't mean we were deprived of love or attention. I always knew my parents loved me. They worked hard for *my* benefit. My grandparents retired when my parents were established within the company. We spent lots of time with them. It's how we work. You spend twenty, thirty years working hard and ensuring the business stays in shape for the next generation. When the next generation is ready, you step down and let them take over.'

'And the cycle starts over again.'

'Exactly.'

The length of time it took Beth to respond made him think he'd finally got through to her.

The mutinous tone when she found her voice dispelled that notion. 'That might have been your experience of boarding school but I refuse to believe that not a single one of the rest of you didn't get homesick. Domenico certainly did.'

'I have already conceded that Domenico was built differently to the rest of us. He never embraced his birth right.'

'You mean he wasn't an indoctrinated robot.'

Feeling his temper start to fray again, Alessio sat up and swung his legs round to rest on the floor. 'Domenico had exactly the same upbringing as me, but he rebelled from a young age, and he rebelled against *everything*.'

'Or maybe he was kicking out because he wanted his parents to be the ones looking after him and not nannies and governesses and the occasional visit from a grandparent. Children need love.'

'And we had it.'

'Didn't you miss your parents even a little bit? Did it *never* bother you that they were too busy working to put you to bed at night?'

'How can you miss something you never had? I knew they loved me and that all their hard work was for my benefit. That was enough for me. I dreamed of the day I was old enough to join them. It will be the same for Dom.'

He heard shuffling behind him and turned his head to find Beth sat upright, cross-legged, under the covers.

'You have no idea how things will be for Dom and, please, none of that "guidance" rubbish.

Your brother had the same guidance as you but it didn't change who he was.'

Beth saw the grimace cross Alessio's face at this latest mention of his detested brother.

Frustration had her grabbing her pillow onto her lap and thumping it. 'Can you stop being so ruddy superior for a minute?'

'I'm not being—'

'Yes you *are*.' She punched the pillow again, wishing for a moment that it was Alessio's face. 'You judge everything by your own standards and experiences, but they're *your* experiences, no one else's, and maybe I'm guilty of the same thing, because I can't bear the thought of Dom waking in the night, needing me, but not being able to reach me. I've been there.' She brushed away a hot tear that spilled out from nowhere. 'I know what it's like to miss someone so much your heart feels punched and bruised from the pain. I won't put Dom through that.'

There was a moment of silence before he cautiously said, 'You are speaking of your parents?'

She wiped another tear and nodded.

He shifted his position to face her properly.

His anger had been replaced by a look she couldn't determine. 'What happened to them?'

She blew out a puff of air. The last time she'd spoken of their death had been with Caroline, fourteen years ago. 'A faulty boiler.'

His brow creased in confusion.

She blew out more air. 'We had a faulty boiler. Dad tried to fix it himself.'

She covered her mouth as an image of her smiling father—he was *always* smiling—floated in her mind: a skinny man, barely older than Beth was now when he died, as daft as a brush but with a heart filled with love for his wife and princess daughter. Time had faded the image in her mind but it had never faded the hole his and her mother's deaths had left in her heart.

'My parents were young when they had me. Teenagers. They never had much money. That's why he tried to fix it himself—there wasn't enough money to pay for a professional. Whatever he did to the boiler caused it. They died in their sleep. Carbon monoxide poisoning.'

Alessio's jaw had clenched while she spoke. She could read nothing in his expression. 'Why weren't you affected by it?'

'I was at a sleepover at a friend's house.'

She squeezed her eyes shut, trying to block the memory of waiting for them to collect her, the concern in her friend's mother's eyes when they hadn't answered her calls, the increasingly frantic banging on the unanswered locked front door after she'd driven Beth home, the flash of lights, the *noise* of the sirens, getting closer to their home... The desperate fear that had clutched at her and the chill she had felt down into the marrow of her bones.

'They said I was lucky,' she whispered. She pulled the pillow to her chest and hugged it tightly. 'I didn't feel lucky. I spent the first year with my foster family praying every night not to wake up so I could be with them.'

The silence that followed this could have been broken by a falling feather.

'Accidenti,' he muttered, before blowing out his own long puff of air. 'I'm sorry. That is a terrible thing.'

There was nothing she could say to counter that. Her life had been destroyed.

'Why did you go into foster care?' he asked. 'Was there no family to take you?'

'No one deemed suitable to care for a nine-year-old girl.' Both her parents had been only children from violent, chaotic households. From the little she remembered having learned before their deaths, they'd been determined to give their daughter a different life from the one they'd endured.

The ache in Alessio's guts made him feel as if he'd been punched by a heavyweight.

His brain burned, a furnace raging through it, his palms clammy.

His relationship with his parents was very different from the one he suspected Beth had had with hers but his mother's death had still hit like a blow. He could barely imagine what it would have been like to lose both his parents together, and at such a young age and in such circumstances.

'It was in your foster home you met Caroline?' he asked in a voice that sounded to his ringing ears as if it were coming from a distance.

Her fingers tightened on the pillow. 'She was fostered a year after me. Her mum died of cancer. She never knew her father. She was the same age as me.' She swallowed. 'She was the best friend I ever had. Foster placements rarely last longer than a couple of years but our foster parents let us live with them until we were both eighteen. They could see what we meant to each other and didn't want to split us up.'

'Are you still in contact with them?' he asked.

'Not really. When we moved out new kids came in that needed their care, and we were too busy enjoying the London life to keep in touch.' She cleared her throat and turned her head to look at him.

The sadness he saw in her eyes landed like another punch in his guts.

'I haven't told you this to manipulate you. I just want you to understand. I couldn't live with myself if Dom was sent away and I let it happen without a fight.'

He reached out and touched her hair, wishing he had the words to take away the pain she had lived through.

'I understand,' he said heavily but his words were a lie.

Alessio had lived thirty-five years without feeling an ounce of the emotion Beth carried in her heart. He'd been taught to be strong, to be detached, to be focussed, and he understood why. Emotions messed with thinking. They made people take paths that were not logical.

Drawing her to him, he closed his eyes at the sigh that escaped her when she rested her head on his chest.

This woman, who'd already lost so much, had been the one to pick up the broken pieces from his brother's death. She'd put her life on hold to care for his brother's child when her heart would have been breaking to lose the woman who'd been more of a sister to her than he and Domenico had ever been as brothers to each other.

And, though he knew it was unfamiliar emotions making him say the words to give Beth comfort, he said them anyway. 'I will put Dom's name on the waiting list so we're guaranteed a place but I'll make a deal with you. When the time comes, the three of us will visit the school. If you and Dom are both happy for him to be sent there, then he goes. If he's not happy to go, then we find another school for him closer to home.'

She tilted her head to look at him, the tiniest furrow in her brow. 'You would do that?'

'All I ask is when we visit it, you keep an open mind.'

The relief that spread across her face pushed out the discomfort in his chest that he was going against all tradition for Beth's peace of mind.

And when she pressed her lips to his, kissed him and wrapped her arms tightly around him, he welcomed the familiar ache that filled him and pushed out the cramping, unfamiliar ache in his chest.

The sick feeling Alessio had woken with the morning before still churned hard in his guts on this, his nephew's first birthday.

He'd taken the day off for it. The surprise and gratitude in Beth's eyes when she'd realised he intended to spend the whole day at home with them had cut through him.

It had to be a lingering echo from listening to her relate the horror of her parents' death.

Her story was no worse than he'd imagined. He'd assumed a car crash or something similar, but it was the pain in her voice at the telling that had crushed his chest.

His beautiful, loving wife had lost everyone she'd cared for.

He recalled their conversation in Club Giroud about his brother's relationship with Caroline and her envy of the love they'd shared.

He looked around the sunny garden. The early autumn sun blazed over the tables spread out and laden with food, and the play equipment that had been installed—the soft ball pits, the sand pits, the huge paddling pools—all things that would ruin the lawn, all things Beth had arranged so their son and his infant cousins could play to their hearts' content.

Their *son*?

Since when had he thought of Dom as anything but his nephew?

He watched one of his cousin's daughters, a toddler called Chiara, waddle to Dom and throw her arms around him, wrestling him to the ground with the force of her clumsy embrace. He watched Beth and Chiara's nanny help them to their unsteady feet. Chiara's parents were too busy chatting with other family members—probably discussing business—to notice.

With eyes that felt as if a filter were being

pulled from them, Alessio took the whole scene in.

Small children playing together, watched over by paid staff and a few grandparents.

No older children. They were at boarding school.

The parents of the children in attendance were ignoring their offspring, drinking wine and discussing business. Most of them would head back to the office when the party was over.

The only parent interacting and playing with the children... Beth.

His beautiful, loving Beth.

For the first time he wondered—really wondered—if the Palvetti way was the right way.

Gina and Marcello suddenly appeared in the garden, arms laden with presents, their own small children trailing behind them holding their nanny's hand. Alessio's instinct was not to stride over, greet them and thank them for Dom's birthday gifts but to shield Beth from Gina's cold stare.

He'd come to a truce with his cousin after she'd apologised to him and assured him of her full support. He had a feeling Marcello had talked her into seeing reason, but the gesture had loosened some of the angst that seemed constantly to be clawing at him.

The gesture did not stop his instinct to gather his wife close to him and protect her.

She didn't need his protection, he thought, watching her smile drop when she spotted Gina. Her shoulders rose before she scooped Dom into her arms and carried him to her. Beth could hold her own.

He hadn't told her about the argument in the boardroom. He'd got his own way, no one had resigned, so what had there been to tell? Beth had thrown herself into the arrangements with all the gusto he remembered from when she'd been organising the ball and he didn't want her to have cause to doubt herself.

Those doubts were on his head.

What if Gina was right? What if opening the doors to their facility led to their ruin?

But, even if she gave him categorical proof that that would be the case, he didn't know if he could stop the wheels that were now in motion. Beth was the happiest he'd ever known her. He couldn't take that from her. He'd taken everything else.

In his arrogance, he'd thought she should be grateful for the chance he was taking by marrying her. He was giving her everything!

But that everything was nothing she wanted.

In his arrogance he'd made her quit the job she loved and give up her flat, and had had the nerve to say and think that she was coming into their marriage with nothing when that nothing was what she'd worked hard for.

She'd *had* to work hard. She'd never had the back-up he'd taken for granted his whole life. No family to turn to if times got hard.

No wonder his family had long ago deduced that marrying for love caused nothing but problems.

And that was his problem. He could deny it no longer. He might as well deny his eyes were green.

He'd fallen in love with his wife.

There was nothing he would not do to make her happy.

And the knowledge of what it would take to give Beth the happiness he wanted for her felt like a spiked fist twisting in his guts.

He had to let her go.

CHAPTER THIRTEEN

ALESSIO ENTERED THE nursery and found Miranda preparing to read a bedtime story to a freshly bathed and fed Dom.

'I'll do that,' he said. 'Come back in fifteen minutes.'

Alone with his nephew, he sat him on his lap and opened the tractor book.

Dom immediately snatched it from his hands and shoved as much of it as he could fit into his mouth.

Alessio laughed even though his heart wasn't in it.

It was hard to feel anything but despair.

He would be leaving with Beth soon for the party at the workshop. This would be the last time he would read his nephew's favourite book to him.

Dom then thrust the book at Alessio's face. 'Ook.'

'What?'

'Ook.'

He gazed into the bright-blue eyes that were so like his dead brother's and wanted to weep.

'Book?' he managed to ask.

Dom beamed, clambered up his uncle's chest and pressed his open mouth to Alessio's cheek in the way he'd seen him do to Beth.

An emotion of such intense purity filled him that, suddenly, Alessio found himself holding Dom tightly in his arms and brushing kisses on the fragile head covered in soft, fluffy blond hair.

He loved this little boy. Loved him so much it hurt his heart.

As soon as he loosened his hold, Dom wriggled and smothered Alessio's face with sloppy kisses, giggling manically.

Dom's needs were as simple as Beth's, he realised with a sharp pain in his chest. Other than the basic necessities, all he needed was love.

It didn't make what he had to do any easier but it fortified his belief that it was the right path to take.

It was the only path to take.

* * *

'Are you *sure*, I look okay?' Beth asked anxiously.

It was the third time she'd asked in as many minutes.

Sensing her nerves were eating at her, and wanting to cut them off before they could come to a head, Alessio left the shoe he was about to put his foot into, strode over and cupped her cheeks in his hands.

'Listen to me,' he said quietly. 'You look beautiful. Your dress is perfect. Your hair is perfect. Nothing is going to go wrong.'

Chocolate eyes gleamed at him before a small smile curved her lips.

In truth, she looked stunning. The long, white off-the-shoulder dress she'd chosen with the deep red roses embellished on its skirt managed to be conservative, sexy and sophisticated all in one. She'd spent the afternoon at a salon and now her hair gleamed and fell in waves around her bare shoulders. The only obvious cosmetics she wore were a deep red lipstick that matched the roses on her dress and the colour painted on her nails. On her feet were dusky pink shoes with gold high heels.

Not wanting to smudge her lipstick and give her something else to worry about, he settled for rubbing his nose to hers. 'Go and say goodnight to Dom.'

The moment the door closed behind her, he shut his eyes, took a long breath and swallowed hard to dislodge the pain in his throat.

What had started as an ache in his heart had steadily turned into a pain that wracked his entire being.

But, whatever pain he had to live with, nothing was worse than the alternative, the selfish alternative, of keeping his wife tied to his side when he knew she could never be truly happy with him, the man who had threatened and blackmailed her into this life.

Sometimes he would look at her and wonder how she could bear his touch, never mind welcome it.

She would welcome her freedom more. That was the conclusion he'd been forced to accept. Mind-blowing sex did not make happiness. Freedom did.

Alessio had always been free to choose his own path. That the path he'd chosen had been preordained had never bothered him at all.

He'd had a lifelong goal and in achieving it he'd thrived.

He'd thrived because he'd never had to feel, not on anything but a superficial level. He'd shed a few tears at his mother's funeral but, as awful as it was to admit it to himself, he'd felt detached from the mourning. He missed her glamorous presence in his life and her often wicked sense of humour but he didn't miss her in the fundamental way Beth still missed her parents fifteen years after their deaths.

His brother had felt. Domenico had felt things deeply. And, rather than try and accept his brother for what he was, Alessio had sneered at him and condemned him for his choices.

He'd been a patronising bastard, he thought painfully. Because Alessio was feeling now. All the things he'd thought he would never feel in his meticulously planned life were there, slicing into his skin and ripping into his heart.

Was it any wonder his brother had turned his back on them?

Beth would never turn her back on them because she would never leave Dom. What kind of freedom was that? What kind of *life* was that? What did riches matter when the heart yearned to be somewhere else?

Beth deserved happiness more than anyone he knew.

Ultimately, he knew that could only come if he set her free. Free to choose her own path. Free to raise Dom as she saw fit. Free to forge a life where she didn't feel like an outsider or judged, disliked or have to mould herself to fit in.

Domenico and Caroline had chosen Beth to raise their child because they had known that, in her care, their child would always be loved and protected. How right they had been.

And now it was Alessio's turn to do the right thing.

The bedroom door burst open and she appeared in the doorway, her brow creased. 'I thought we had to go?'

Muttering an apology, he put on his shoes.

When he got to his feet she'd come close to him and was looking at him intently.

'Are you okay?' she asked.

His chest rose. Brushing his thumb down her cheek for what could be the last time, he nodded. 'Come. Let us show my family exactly what you are made of.'

Beth could hardly believe the past four weeks of meticulous planning and hard work was coming to fruition.

A party for ten—twenty if you counted partners, which she did—had involved almost the same amount of work as for the masquerade ball's four hundred guests.

The planning for this party had different challenges and intricacies, and far more complications than the ball, but she had loved every minute of it.

Yet now, when she should be suffering the nerves that normally took hold of her at this time, her attention was fixed solely on Alessio, whose own attention was fixed firmly on the view from his window seat of the helicopter.

She wished she could ask again what was wrong with him but sharing the cabin with them were Gina and Marcello. She was so concerned about her husband that she didn't even bother to worry if Gina was having poisonous thoughts towards her.

Something was wrong. She was certain of it.

It was a feeling that had been growing these past few weeks and had crystallised when she'd walked into the bedroom and found him sat on the sofa with an expression on his face she'd never seen before.

He'd looked ill.

The one thing she'd been able to rely on since they'd married was their mutual desire for each other but even in the bedroom she'd sensed changes happening. Alessio still made love with the same intensity but he'd stopped reaching for her in his sleep. That was, if he even slept. She was certain he was awake when she drifted off and she couldn't remember the last time she'd woken to find him lying beside her. Dom's birthday, maybe.

They hadn't spent as much time together as they normally did either. He rarely dropped by her office.

Then there had been the many hours she'd spent at the facility itself, preparing for the party. She'd been touched when he'd suggested she take Dom there with her but it had pained her that Alessio had made excuses and stayed behind. While this further proof of his faith in her should delight her, all it did was trouble her. It felt as though he was slipping away.

There had been days when she'd hardly seen her husband.

Had he sensed her changed feelings towards him? Was that why he was being so distant with her?

Madness or not, she loved him. Denying it was pointless.

She loved him.

She'd tried desperately hard not to let her feelings show but there were times she ached to tell him the truth, to lay her cards out before him and see where it would lead.

And then the voice of sanity would prevail. Alessio would be horrified if he knew how deeply her feelings for him ran.

Wouldn't he?

She didn't dare believe that all the little things he did to put her needs first, such as insisting that she finish work at a decent time so she could be home for Dom's dinner, as he'd done in recent weeks, actually meant something deeper to him.

She pushed her worries aside when she saw the lights of the monastery in the distance.

With summer over and the early autumn nights drawing in, she'd timed it so the guests would arrive when the sky was dark. This meant she could use the theatricality of the location to its best advantage. She'd insisted on having white fairy lights installed along the perimeter of the roof and along the trees that traversed the entire complex, and white night lights running the length of the driveway to it, so their guests would see it in all its beauty when the helicopters brought them in to land.

'It looks beautiful.'

The murmured compliment came from Gina.

When they landed, the first limousine drove up so they could enter it without hardly having to touch the earth with their feet.

Rather than get in, Beth hurried to the other limousines in the row and quickly checked each had the bottle of champagne on ice and champagne flutes that she'd ordered.

'You are worried?' Gina asked when she joined them in the waiting car for the half-mile journey to the complex itself.

'A little,' she admitted. 'I always get like this before an event.'

She waited for the cutting remark that was

sure to follow and was pleasantly surprised when Gina simply said, 'Try and relax. Your preparations have been meticulous.'

When they entered the reception room, they stepped through the new walk-through electronic scanner purchased especially for the occasion. Beth had figured their guests, which included royalty, would not be impressed to have hand-held scanners checking their bodies for illicit technology.

The last-minute checks were done and then word came that the first helicopter had landed.

It was time for the show to begin.

Alessio had known that with Beth in charge of the planning the event was bound to be a success, but he had not envisaged quite how well it would go.

Their elite number of guests, puffed up with importance at being the select few, couldn't quite hide that they felt like children in a chocolate factory.

Once the tour of the laboratories was over— and somehow his clever wife had arranged that to flow like a piece of performing art—they were settled in the meeting room which had been transformed beyond recognition.

Thick gold velvet drapes covered the walls, crystal chandeliers now hung on the ceiling and plump sofas lay strategically for weary feet to rest, giving the room a rich, sparkling intimacy. The abundance of canapés and free-flowing drinks were served by specially hired models who were the epitome of elegance, all wearing identical silver outfits and Palvetti jewellery. The string quartet played familiar classical tunes at just the right noise level to allow unhampered conversation.

A small scream suddenly resounded from the far corner, followed by the roar of laughter. One of the guests had not realised the beautiful gold statues in each corner were in fact real humans who changed their positions slightly, in time, every ten minutes.

And Beth played her part perfectly too, a gracious, welcoming hostess with the beauty to charm the men and an innate friendliness for the women to warm to. Right then, she was talking to his old friend Giannis Basinas's date for the evening.

As if sensing Alessio's gaze on her, Beth turned her head to look at him.

His heart thumped.

Their gazes held.

If he lived to be one hundred, he would never tire of looking at her.

After tonight there was a chance he would never see her again.

By the end of the night, it would all be over.

He'd been selfish, he knew, not setting her free sooner but he'd wanted her to have this night.

He hoped that, when time eventually healed the new hurts he was going to inflict on her, her abiding memory of their marriage would be of this night: her triumph.

'Was the date Giannis brought tonight the woman he spent the night of the masquerade ball dancing with?' Beth asked, even though she already knew the answer.

Since they'd got out of the helicopter and said goodbye to Gina and Marcello to take the drive to their respective homes in their own cars, Alessio hadn't said one word to her.

He hadn't looked at her.

'She might have been.' His lack of interest was obvious.

'You never did tell me what the favour was you did all those years ago that was big enough that he agreed to hold the masquerade ball for you.'

She caught the tiniest quirk on his lips through the moonlight pouring through the car window.

'He glued the headmaster's office furniture to the floor. All of it. And all his stationery to his desk and all his books to the shelves of the cabinet. I provided the alibi that stopped him being expelled.'

She laughed, not because she thought it funny—although on any other occasion she would have found it hilarious—but because she thought it an appropriate response. She'd spent the whole night thinking of appropriate responses when speaking to their elite guests and she had the same nerves in her stomach now as she did then. 'Why did he do that?'

He gave a small shrug. 'One of the other kids dared him.'

The driver slowed for the gates to their estate to open.

Beth couldn't think of another thing to say to cut the tension for the last minute of this excruciating journey.

She was used to a lack of affection in their business life—that one mind-blowing, frantic coupling on her desk excepted—but he was never cold with her.

Right then she feared if she touched him she would get frostbite.

Thuds of dread hammered in her chest when she followed him up the winding staircase to their quarters.

'I'm just going to check on Dom,' she murmured when they reached their bedroom door.

'Leave it for a minute,' he commanded. 'I have something to discuss with you.'

'I'll just be a—'

'No. This cannot wait.'

He opened the door and waited for her to step into the bedroom.

The thuds of her heart had become so loud, they pounded through her bones.

He walked straight to his bureau and opened a drawer. From it he pulled a bottle of Scotch.

'I thought you didn't drink in the bedroom.'

'I had this ready.'

'It's that bad, is it?'

'No. It isn't bad. Sit with me.'

He poured them both a measure and handed a glass to her, then they sat on the long sofa that ran the length of the wall beneath the windows. Beth noticed he kept a safe distance from her.

Her hands shook as she raised the glass to her lips.

His hands didn't seem much more together.

Alessio took a large drink and grimaced.

It was time.

'Beth, there is no easy way for me to say this, so I will get straight to the point.'

She flinched before he could go any further. 'Have I done something wrong?'

How could she think that even for a second?

'No. You have done your best, but I can't see a viable role for you here any more. The party tonight was a one-off that will never be repeated.' He hated lying to her. Only the knowledge that it had to be this way gave him the strength to continue. 'I should never have allowed you to host it. I took a risk that seems to have paid off but I cannot risk it again—the security implications are too great.'

'Then what do you envisage me doing?'

'Nothing.' His guts clenched at this second blatant lie.

Beth had the potential to be the greatest asset Palvetti had ever had. But she was not an asset. She was a woman of flesh and blood with a heart that deserved to love and be loved.

She deserved to find the love she so longed for.

'Nothing? Are you firing me?'

Alessio kneaded his forehead. He'd gone over and over this moment in his mind so many times that the speech he'd prepared should have fallen from his tongue easily and left them both with their pride and dignity intact but it had already slipped away from him.

'There is no role for you to play within the business. You are free to leave.'

He braced himself for her to jump to her feet and start dancing with glee.

'That's not funny.'

'It's not meant to be.'

Her nose wrinkled. 'What am I supposed to do? Be a full-time mum? In theory that's lovely but I've got used to working again. I'm not a fan of the long hours so I could do something part-time. That would give me the best of both worlds, wouldn't it? Do you want me to work directly for you as an assistant—?'

'You are not listening,' he interrupted, his tone harsher than he wanted. 'You will not be returning to work with me. I thought I could make it work and that I could mould you into a Palvetti but I was wrong. If there is no role for you to play within the business, then there is no role for you to play in my life. Our marriage is over.'

Silence rang out between them.

Her voice, when she finally responded, was quiet. 'When you say over...do you mean divorce?'

'Yes.'

Confusion was written all over her beautiful face. 'But Palvettis don't divorce.'

'We don't marry strangers into our family either, but I did with you.'

'But...' Her mouth opened and closed. She shook her head and blinked a number of times. 'Are you serious?'

He strove to keep his tone neutral and matter-of-fact. 'I've had the staff pack your possessions for you—they've been put in your old room by Dom's nursery. You can sleep there tonight. In the morning you can take my jet and fly wherever you want. Your life is yours to live again as you see fit.'

'But… I don't understand. What have I done? I must have done something.'

'You haven't done anything wrong.' He could not stress that enough. He would not have her think she was in any way to blame for this whole rotten mess. 'You have many great qualities but I've never made any pretence over what I need in a wife. I need a business partner. You are not that woman.'

Not a wife for whom he played games of risk with his family business to make happy.

That was the thought he needed to add strength to his resolve.

Never in his life had he put anyone or anything above the business, not even his own brother. And why? Because he'd been a selfish, tunnel-visioned bastard.

For once in his life he was going to do the right thing.

For Beth he would do anything. She'd suffered enough in her life. He would not put her through any more, however much it shredded his heart to let her go.

Her eyes were wide. 'You want to marry someone else?'

No. Never. Beth was the only woman he wanted. He loved her. He loved her more than life itself. He would give up everything for her and that meant giving her up. She needed to be free to find the love she had longed for before he'd destroyed her life. How could he ever be that man after what he'd done to her?

Why was she still here? Why hadn't she snatched her freedom the moment he'd said she had it? Had she become so indoctrinated into his world that she couldn't see outside it any more?

It was down to him to sever that indoctrination once and for all.

He did not drop his gaze from hers or allow any of the emotions ripping through his chest to show on his face. 'I want a wife who will fit in.'

He'd never seen her face so pale.

'You cold bastard,' she whispered.

'Yes.'

'This has all been for nothing?' Her voice rose a notch. 'I've given up my job and my home for *nothing*? And what about Dom? If you divorce me, I get custody of him. Or did you forget that?'

Dom was part of the reason he was doing this. That little orphaned boy deserved all the love his parents would have lavished on him. Only Beth could give him that.

'I didn't forget. I will pay for whatever education you feel is right for him, and pay for his upkeep and give you enough money for yourself that you need never work again. I'll buy you a house in your name to raise him in. He can visit me as he grows up and, if he decides when he's an adult that he wants to be a part of this world, then I will welcome him into it.'

Cradling her untouched glass, she slowly got to her feet.

She walked a few paces then turned around to face him.

Her stare was accusatory. 'You've got it all figured out. You're that keen to get rid of me that you're prepared to lose the whole reason you brought me here?'

'It's for the best.' He raised his shoulders. 'I want you to be happy, *bella*, but how can you be happy in this world? You said yourself that you're not a good fit for us. You find the business and my family overwhelming and—'

'Don't try and make this about me. This is all about *you*. I gave up everything for you.'

'You gave it up for Dom.'

'That's because I love him and would do anything for him, something you wouldn't understand, because you're incapable of love. I thought you were growing to love him too but I got that wrong like I got everything else wrong. I've bent over backwards trying to fit in and carve a niche for myself in your world, and all along you were watching me fail and stringing me along and deciding, "oops, I made a mistake, I don't want you to be my wife after all! I want someone better because you're not worth it".'

'I have never thought that.'

'Do not insult my intelligence… Actually, go ahead and insult it. I've already insulted it myself, swallowing all your lies, when I knew from the start the kind of man you were. Domenico was right all along, wasn't he? I thought he'd got it wrong and that beneath the skin was a decent human being who I…' She cut herself off and took a deep breath. When she next fixed her eyes on him, venom spilled from them. 'All you care about is the business. Everything else can go to hell as far you're concerned, can't it? Well, I tell you this much: you're the one who's going to be going to hell for this.'

Magnificent in her fury, she stormed to the bedroom door. 'I'm going to get Dom. I won't spend another night under this roof.'

'It's the middle of the night. Let him sleep.'

She pointed her finger at him, her face screwed up in pain and rage. '*Don't* pretend to care about him. Don't you dare. If you cared an ounce for him you would have left us both where we were in London and never dragged us into this cruel game of yours.'

'Beth...' Everything inside him was twisted and torn. He hated to see her anger writ large but knew he deserved it. He deserved every ounce of her hate. It was only for Dom's sake that she'd kept her true feelings buried inside her all this time. 'I'm sorry.'

Her response was to turn her back and walk out of the room.

Breathing heavily, Alessio bit back the almost overwhelming compulsion to run after her.

He'd achieved what he'd set out to do. He'd set her free.

That her freedom came at the expense of his own shattering heart was no one's fault but his own.

CHAPTER FOURTEEN

BETH LOOKED AT her watch again and sighed.
She'd been sat in the airport's private lounge for
three hours. There'd been an accident on one
of Milan's bypasses and the pilot was stuck in
the resulting traffic.

Her phone vibrated.

It was a message from Miranda asking if she
was okay.

Beth sighed again and rubbed her eyes. She
felt so tired.

She'd been full of so much anger and pain
when she'd gone into the nursery, intent on
snatching Dom from his cot and leaving straight
away, but then she'd seen his tiny sleeping form
and had known it would take a heart as cold as
the man she'd married to wake him.

So she'd lain by his cot, unwilling to get into
the bed she'd first slept in those first nights in
Milan that felt so far away now, and waited

until he'd stirred. She'd dressed him first then rifled through one of the cases the staff had put for her in her old room and changed into jeans and a light jumper.

The sun had only just risen when she'd left the villa in a cab.

Other than Miranda, who had appeared like a ghost as she'd left the nursery—the look on her face showing she was in the know about the...what to call it? Split? Separation? Severing of her heart? She saw no one.

Dom, currently in a high chair, threw a bit of the croissant she'd broken into pieces for him onto the floor.

Hot tears stabbed the back of her eyes as she stared at his happy little face and wondered how Alessio could give up on him like this.

She knew the reason why. It was because he didn't want *her*. She didn't fit in.

She'd been right about that from the start.

And she'd been right not to hope that all those thoughtful things he'd done for her had been because he'd developed actual feelings for her as a woman and lover rather than just seeing her as a business spouse.

A sudden tightness in her chest doubled her over.

She put a hand to her heart, grabbed a hank of hair with the other and pulled hard but the tightness in her chest clenched even more and she gasped for breath.

How could he *do* this? How could he just turn around and let them go as if they meant nothing to him?

He didn't want her. He wanted to marry someone else, a woman who would seamlessly fit into his life and be happy with whatever role she was given.

His words floated in her head. *I want you to be happy,* bella...

She inhaled deeply through her nose and thought hard to recall everything he'd said.

What had he meant about there being no *viable* role for her within Palvetti? Literally the only jobs that couldn't be catered for within it were for musicians and actors. And maybe social media gurus. Other than that, a niche could be found for everyone.

So why not for her?

And why let Dom go?

That was the one thing that made no sense.

Dom was the entire reason he'd married her. He'd wanted his nephew to take his place in the family, to be groomed to potentially one day run the business. Everything was about the business. It was how the Palvettis worked. It was their very reason for being.

For all Alessio knew, she could take Dom right now and go into hiding somewhere where Alessio would never find them.

Her heart suddenly starting to thrum, she leaned under the table to pick the plastic cup of water Dom had decided to throw onto the floor, probably aiming at the mess of croissant crumbs already there—thankfully the cup had a lid—and, as she gave it back to him, her phone rang.

Thinking it must be Miranda, whose text she still hadn't responded to, she was taken aback to see Gina's name flash on the screen.

Alessio had programmed all the directors' numbers into her phone ages ago. Not one of them had ever called her on it.

She debated with herself for a moment then tentatively put it to her ear. 'Hello?'

'Beth? It's Gina.'

'Hi...'

'I just want to congratulate you.'

'For what?'

'The party.' Gina laughed. It even sounded genuine. 'It was a masterstroke. You did an incredible job.'

Beth was so surprised at the compliments that it took her a moment to respond. 'Thank you.'

The pitch of Gina's voice lowered. 'I owe you an apology.'

'Oh?'

'I haven't behaved well towards you and for that I'm sorry. And while I'm here apologising I should say I'm sorry for doubting you about the party too. I should have trusted Alessio's judgement. He shouldn't have had to threaten to resign over it.'

Blood rushed to Beth's head, dizzying her. Alessio had threatened to *resign*?

'Beth? Are you there?'

'Sorry,' she murmured, her thoughts far away.

'I thought I'd lost you. *Va bene*, I need to go. I'll see you in the morning. *Ciao*.'

'*Ciao*, Gina,' she whispered.

She placed her phone on the table and stared at her little boy, trying desperately to make sense of the short conversation.

She sat there for ages, lost in thought, trying to fit the pieces of the jigsaw together, knowing she *must* fit them…just as she'd tried to fit herself into the Palvetti mould.

Alessio had told her she didn't fit in the Palvetti mould.

If he felt that strongly about it—strongly enough to end their marriage and lose custody of Dom over it—then why had he stuck his neck out and threatened to walk away from the business over the party?

Her phone rang again.

It was the cabin crew. The pilot had arrived.

It was time to leave Milan and pick up the pieces of her old life.

It was time to reclaim her freedom.

Alessio sat on the sun-faded sofa that hadn't been used in four years and bowed his head.

Music rang out through the speakers piped throughout the ground floor, connecting from his brother's studio where Alessio had turned on the sound system. That had been unused for four years too.

He closed his eyes and let the raw music envelop him.

It did nothing to dull the wrenching pain in his heart.

Beth had been right. His brother did have talent.

Alessio had been too…what was the word she'd used that time? Superior? It fitted. He'd been too superior in his judgement of his brother to bother to listen to the music Domenico had created.

He wished he'd listened to it when he'd been alive.

He wished he hadn't waited until their mother had died to track him down. If he'd overridden his pride there might have been a rapprochement. Unlikely, he knew. The scars of their childhood had run deep in Domenico.

He wished he hadn't been so dismissive of his brother's feelings.

He wished a lot of things that could never be.

He could never make things right with his brother but at least he was now, finally, doing right by his son.

Beth would care for Dom as she had always done, with that fierce protectiveness and a world full of love.

He covered his face with his hands and bowed his head.

They would be back in England now, ready to embrace a new chapter in their lives where they could live with freedom.

The wrenching pain in his heart twisted into a vice that hurt so much, he groaned with the agony of it.

Digging his fingers into his skull, he could hold the tears back no longer.

For the first time in his life, Alessio wept.

He wept for the loss of the child he'd grown to love with all his heart.

And he wept for the loss of the woman who had taken possession of that same heart.

Alone in the cottage that had belonged to the brother he'd rejected, he cried until there were no tears left to cry.

Where was he?

No one had seen him.

If he'd left the grounds, he hadn't taken one of the cars. He *had* to be here. Somewhere.

Leaving Dom with Miranda, who'd been packing her possessions together when Beth had made her scream with fright by walking into the nursery, she left the villa and went in search of him.

Her heart thumped and her lungs felt tight as she trawled the great garden, the greenhouses, the summer house, all empty of human life.

Where was he?

She suddenly caught a glimpse of the lakeside cottage in the distance.

She stared at it for the longest time before setting one foot in front of the other.

Why was she even here?

That was a question to which she still didn't fully know the answer.

After she'd received the call to say she could board the plane, she'd put Dom into his buggy—he'd outgrown the pram in his months in Milan—and walked through the airport lounge door but, instead of taking the route to the plane, she'd taken the route to the car park and climbed into the first available cab.

Not until she reached the cottage door did she understand why she'd come back.

She turned the handle. There was no resistance. The door was unlocked.

She stepped inside.

Dust swirled in a haze before her but she

hardly registered it for the figure slumped on the faded sofa.

Bloodshot eyes met hers, held for a moment then closed.

Then they snapped back open again.

Slowly he sat upright. 'Beth?'

But her heart had thumped so hard to see him it had caught in her throat.

'What are you doing here?' he asked thickly.

She swallowed hard and fought for a breath. 'I have a question for you.'

He unfurled his body some more. 'You came back…to ask me a question?'

'One question.'

He rose to his feet.

She took in the crumpled, untucked shirt and the charcoal trousers. He'd worn those clothes to the party.

She took in the puffiness around the bloodshot eyes. The untamed black curls. The thick stubble.

The lump in her throat and the tightness in her lungs loosened a touch.

He jerked a nod. 'One question.'

'You have to answer it honestly.'

His eyes narrowed slightly. *'Va bene.'*

'Do you have feelings for me?'

His jaw clenched and he looked away from her. 'Ask something else.'

'That's my question.'

His face had become a mask.

'That's my question. I'm not leaving until you answer it.'

But he didn't. He simply stared at the wall with that clenched yet expressionless look, hiding any feelings he might have away, out of sight.

She could bear it no longer. She walked up to him and stared right into his face until he was forced to look at her.

'Will you answer my question?' she beseeched. 'Surely you owe me that much? After everything you've done to me, the least you can do is tell me if you have any kind of feelings for me.'

He went from still to motion without warning. Suddenly he had her shoulders in his grip and his face just inches from her. 'Yes,' he snarled, emerald eyes boring into hers, 'I have feelings for you. Is that what you want to hear? And, now you've heard it, you can leave.'

Alessio released his hold as suddenly as he'd taken it.

Why had she come back?

He could howl at the despair rising in him at her failure to grasp the freedom he'd given her.

He should never have taken it in the first place.

'What kind of feelings?' she whispered. '*Tell me.*'

'What does it matter?'

'It matters to me.'

'Beth...' He gritted his teeth and prayed for strength. 'I have lied. I have deceived. I have blackmailed. I have done so many terrible things to you that I know when I meet my maker it will be Satan waiting for me. What I feel for you is not important. *You're* what's important. You don't deserve this life that I forced on you. You deserve happiness...every happiness. I wish that could be with me but I know it can't. I've taken everything from you. My brother was right to want to keep his child from me. I'm selfish. I think only of what's best for the business and not the person before me. For once in my life, I am trying to do the right thing for another person—for you. And your son. Dom *is* your son. I should never have threatened to take him from you.'

His legs couldn't hold him up any longer. He sank onto the sofa and rubbed his head in his hands.

'Then why did you say you...?' there was a catch in her voice '...you...wanted to marry another woman?'

Desolation filled him. 'All lies. You wouldn't leave. You wouldn't listen. You're still not listening. Please, for the love of God, *go.*'

He jolted when warm fingers wrapped around his hands and moved them from his face.

Lifting his head, he found her crouched before him, her beautiful face staring intently at him.

The chocolate eyes were soft on his. 'Do you love me?'

Despair rose back up in him. 'You need to ask?'

'No. But I need to hear it.'

'Why?'

She shifted her stance so her knees rested between his feet, moved her hands lightly up his arms and placed the palms on his chest. The tiniest smile curved on her full lips. 'I can feel your heart beat.'

He smothered a groan. His heart was beating so hard he could feel the beats echoing in his pounding head.

Keeping one hand on his chest, she moved the other to rest at the base of his throat.

'When my parents died, I didn't just lose them. I lost the only home I'd known, my school, all my friends...'

He breathed deeply, listening intently, even through the sick prickles of awareness growing at her touch.

'I was moved to a foster home fifty miles away. The couple who fostered me had two children of their own. They were a nice family and they looked after me very well but I never felt a part of *them*. Do you understand what I'm saying?'

He shook his head. How could he understand *anything* of what she'd lived through?

'When we went out, they held their own children's hands. They rarely held mine. I would get a peck on the top of my head as a goodnight kiss where they would literally smother their children with kisses. I felt excluded from their affection. Their home never felt like mine. It couldn't. There was always a time limit to it. I felt wanted by them, but I never felt their love, not in the way they showed it to their children or the way my parents had showed it to me.

'When Caroline moved in with us she'd just lost her mother. I'd just reached the point where I accepted my parents were really gone, so I did what felt natural and took care of her through her grief, and that's how our relationship stayed—I was only three months older but I became the big sister.'

The hand on his chest drifted up to palm his cheek.

'You are the first person to have put my happiness first since my parents died.'

His heart lurched violently.

'Yes, you lied at the beginning and blackmailed me, but since then you have gone out of your way to make things good for me. My happiness matters to you. My fulfilment matters to you. *I* matter to you. You've proved that in so many different ways.'

He couldn't breathe.

She brought her face closer to his. Her warm breath breezed against his cheek. 'I know you threatened to resign from the company over the party.'

'Beth...'

Her lips brushed softly against his, silencing him.

'I have spent the past fifteen years aching for love but being terrified of finding it. Life is fragile. Those I've loved have either died or been unable to return it in the way I needed.'

She pulled her head back enough so that she could stare deep into his eyes. 'I came to your home feeling like a fish out of water. I saw the riches you surround yourself with, I saw the sophistication of your life and I thought it would be impossible for me to fit in. I saw your family as a bunch of icebergs. Do you know what I see now?'

He shook his head slowly.

'I see a family who show love differently to what I thought was normal. I accused you once of judging everyone by your own standards— well, I was just as guilty. And do you know what I feel when I walk into your villa now?'

He swallowed and shook his head again.

'I feel home. *Home.*' Tears filled her eyes and her voice dropped so low he had to strain to hear the words. 'I have not felt like I've had a home since I was nine years old. *You* did that for me, Alessio. You brought me into your world and you made sure I felt a part of it.

'Last night you gave me my freedom back. I can take Dom anywhere I want and live my life any way I choose.' Her lips caressed his again then brushed across his cheek, a teardrop falling onto it to rest against his ear. 'I choose you.'

Those three words sent his head and his senses reeling.

She chose him. Beth chose him.

With her own free will, Beth chose him.

Finally, he allowed himself to touch her. He wrapped his arms around her and pulled her to him until he had her pinned to his lap and it was his hands cradling her cheeks.

He gazed at the face he would love until his dying breath and a surge of wonder ripped through him. 'I love you,' he said quietly. 'I love you more than I thought it was possible to love someone. There is nothing I wouldn't do for you and nothing I wouldn't do for Dom. I don't want him to have the childhood I had. I want him to have the childhood my brother wished for him. I promise I will do everything in my power to be the husband and father you both deserve. I will cut down on the hours I work. No more weekends. You've made me see that, as important as the business is, our family—you, me and Dom—is more important than anything. You come first. I would give up everything for you.'

There were so many emotions engulfing Beth that for a long time she couldn't say anything.

She'd said all she needed to say. Apart from one last thing.

'I love you.' And she loved the way those emerald eyes pulsed as she said those words. Joy careering through her at such speed it made her dizzy, she said them again. 'I love *you.*'

He gazed into her eyes for one more long, lingering moment before his mouth crushed hers and they expressed their love for each other with so much more than words.

EPILOGUE

'ARE YOU SURE I look okay?'

Alessio looked up from the sleeve of his shirt where he was fastening a cufflink and stared with unadorned wonder at his wife.

In a long, red silk dress that skimmed her growing cleavage and hugged her swelling stomach, she looked ravishing.

'You, *bella*, look good enough to eat.'

Her eyes gleamed at the suggestiveness of his tone.

He'd always thought the saying about pregnant women glowing was a myth. His wife had proved it true and in this, her second pregnancy, she had never looked more beautiful.

Their bedroom door was barged open and four-year-old Dom walked in carrying two-year-old Bruno under Bruno's armpits.

'Put him down,' Beth scolded kindly. 'He's not a pet.'

Dom let go. Luckily there wasn't far for Bruno

to fall and he landed with a small flump on his bottom.

Immediately he held his arms up for his big brother to pick him up again.

Alessio saved him the bother, lifting them with one arm each and depositing them on the bed. 'Where's Miranda?'

'Getting our milk. Can we come with you, Babbo?'

It never failed to make Alessio's heart burst to hear Dom call him that: Daddy.

And he *was* his daddy, in every way possible. Two months after Beth had learned she was pregnant with Bruno, they'd legally adopted Dom. He was theirs. They loved him. They might not be his biological parents but they were his mummy and daddy.

He rubbed Dom's hair. 'Not tonight, *topolina*. Mummy's hosting an important party at our facility in Lake Como.'

Their first select party had proven to be the best marketing event Palvetti had ever undertaken. Word in select circles had spread like wildfire and commissions had rocketed. It had unanimously been agreed to make it an annual event and unanimously agreed that Beth would run it. For three months a year she dedicated her time to organising the party. The rest of the time she did as she pleased, helping out on projects if anyone asked, but mostly enjoying her time with the children.

She would be able to enjoy her time with them for as long as she wanted. Dom's name had been removed from the Quilton House waiting list. None of their children would go to boarding school.

Gathering his boys into his arms, he carried them to Beth so they could ruin her make-up with their sloppy kisses, then carried them back to the nursery.

* * * * *

LET'S TALK
Romance

For exclusive extracts, competitions
and special offers, find us online:

f facebook.com/millsandboon

⊙ @millsandboonuk

🐦 @millsandboon

Or get in touch on 0844 844 1351*

For all the latest titles coming soon,
visit millsandboon.co.uk/nextmonth

*Calls cost 7p per minute plus your phone company's price per
minute access charge